SECOND HARVEST

JEAN GIONO (1895–1970) was born in Manosque, Provence, the son of an Italian cobbler, and lived there most of his life. He supported his family working as a bank clerk for eighteen years (with an interval serving in the ranks in the First World War) before his first two novels were published, thanks to the generosity of André Gide, to critical acclaim. He went on to write thirty novels and numerous essays and stories, as well as poetry and plays. In 1953 he was awarded the Prix Monégasque for his collective work. The same year, he made a prescient contribution to the "ecological" movement with his novella *The Man who Planted Trees*. This, and his novel *The Horseman on the Roof*, which was made into a highly acclaimed film starring Olivier Martinez and Juliette Binoche, are among this author's titles also published by Harvill. Jean Giono married in 1920 and had two daughters.

Also by Jean Giono in English translation

THE HORSEMAN ON THE ROOF
ANGELO
THE MAN WHO PLANTED TREES

SECOND HARVEST

JEAN GIONO

Translated from the French
by Henri Fluchère and Geoffrey Myers
Illustrated with woodcuts
by Louis William Graux

THE HARVILL PRESS
LONDON

First published with the title *Regain*
by Editions Bernard Grasset, Paris, 1930

First published in Great Britain in 1999 by
The Harvill Press,
2 Aztec Row, Berners Road,
London N1 0PW

www.harvill-press.com

3 5 7 9 8 6 4 2

A CIP catalogue record for this book
is available from the British Library

ISBN 1 86046 266 9

Designed and typeset in Minion at
Libanus Press, Marlborough, Wiltshire

Printed and bound in Great Britain by Butler & Tanner Ltd
at Selwood Printing, Burgess Hill

SECOND HARVEST

PART ONE

I

WHEN THE BANON MAIL-COACH CALLS AT VACHÈRES, it's always about noon.

You may well leave Manosque later, on the days when the usual passengers keep the coach waiting – when you reach Vachères, it's always noon.

It's as regular as clockwork.

It's even rather annoying to arrive there at the same time every day.

Michel, the coach-driver, once tried to stop at the crossroads of Revest-des-Brousses and spin a yarn with Fanette Chabassut, who keeps the Two Monkeys Inn, before setting out again at a leisurely pace. It made no difference. He just wanted to see; well, he did see!

Soon after the turning at the hospital, you notice a blue steeple like a flower rising from the woods. A moment or two later, its big bell starts sounding the angelus with the clangour of a goat-bell.

"Why, it's twelve again!" says Michel, and then, leaning over the old coach-box:

3

"D'you hear that, in there? It's twelve again. Can't do anything about it!"

So the passengers naturally bring out their baskets from under the seats and begin to eat.

Somebody taps on the pane.

"Michel, d'you want some of this good sausage?"

"How about an egg?"

"A bit of cheese?"

"Don't stand on ceremony!"

Michel does not want to offend anybody, so he opens the window and takes everything that is handed to him.

"Wait a bit! Wait a bit! You're overloading me!" He puts the whole lot beside him on his box.

"I'd be glad of a mouthful of bread with it . . . and if anybody happens to have a bottle . . . ."

After Vachères, the road goes uphill.

Here, Michel ties the reins to the brake handle and begins to eat in comfort, leaving the horses to go as they please.

The passengers inside are nearly always the same: a lavender-dealer from the coast towns, a man called Camous or something like that; a shepherd going up to his pastures, who regularly cuts off a chunk of his bread for himself and another for his dog; a farmer's wife all in her Sunday best; and one of those peasant girls who are like simple flowers, with a touch of cornflower-blue in their eyes. Sometimes the tax-collector and his portfolio are also there, sitting side by side like two proper persons.

The Vachères steeple is all blue. It had been distempered from the sacristy right up to its little iron cap. It was an idea of a gentleman who owned the Sylvabelle estate. He refused to drop it.

"But I tell you I myself will pay for the painting, for the whole lot! And also for the painter! I tell you that you won't have to pay for anything and that I'll pay for everything . . . ."

So they let him have his own way. It is not so bad and, at any rate, it can be seen from a long way off.

The passengers in the mail-coach always gaze at this blue steeple while chewing their mouthful of sausage. They look at it for a long time because it is the last steeple seen before entering the wood, and because from there onward the landscape really changes.

It's like this: from Manosque to Vachères there is one hill after another. You go up one side and down the other. But at every hill you go down a little less than you went up. That way, little by little, the ground raises you up without appearing to do so. Those who have already made the journey two or three times realize it, first because at a given moment there are no more fields of vegetables, then because the wheat becomes shorter and shorter, then because they pass under the first chestnut trees, then because they have to ford torrents of grass-coloured water, as shiny as oil, and finally because they see the blue stem of the Vachères steeple, which marks a natural boundary. They know that the hill which begins there is the longest, the stiffest, and the last; and that in one stretch it will carry horses, coach, and people up into the open sky, among wind and clouds. There is no road down on the other side. First you go up through a wood, then across land gnawed by leprosy, like an old bitch losing her hair. Then you find yourself so high that you are buffeted on the shoulders as if by wings, and at the same time you hear the rumble of the ever-blowing wind. Finally you reach the plateau, with its whole surface smoothed down by the gigantic plane of the wind, and then, after a short quarter-hour's trot, in a gentle hollow where the ground has sunk under the weight of a convent and fifty houses, you reach Banon.

The horses are accustomed to it. They first come to a fine bend, like an elbow. As they strain their withers, their collar-bells ring out: first the deep tones from the brown horse and then the tinkling sounds from the white horse – "Your pull, my pull, your pull, my pull . . . " – then the track slants off towards a cluster of chestnut trees and the horses draw up of their own accord.

Michel jumps down from his seat, opens the door, and asks the passengers to alight.

"Ladies and gentlemen, just to rest the horses . . . ."

It happened that Mademoiselle Delphine of the tobacco shop was there that day. So was plump Laure Duvernet, who was on her way to the Glorias farm to help with the pig-killing, and so was

5

Uncle Joseph. As they jumped out onto the road, they said: "You wretch! Making us get out in such weather!"

The oak leaves, like a cantering herd, were swept along by the November wind. It was a hard, dry wind, cold through and through. It had silenced all the brooks at one stroke. There was nothing but its own noise in the wood.

"What, just for a blow of wind!" Michel answered.

Uncle Joseph was the oldest.

"It'll do you good to walk a bit, Uncle," said Michel.

Joseph was the uncle of Agathange, the man who ran the club café at Banon. He was usually to be found in the café near the stove or watching a game of manille, and that is how he became everybody's uncle.

"To talk of doing me good . . . "

"Why, you're feeling quite fit, aren't you?"

"Yes, I shouldn't complain."

"You did well to go and live with your nephew. That was no life for you any more, up there at Aubignane."

"It was hardly habitable. Only five of us were left; then Félippe got his job as postman at Revest. After that I said to myself: 'What are you messing around here for? One of these days the whole lot'll crash down on you. Clear out!' It was about then that I sent word to my nephew. I gave him everything. I'm content with a little soup and tobacco. I manage all right like that."

"And the others, are they still up there?"

"I had news of them from a man on the plateau. Three of them are still up there. There's Gaubert; you know, the wagtail, the father of the Gaubert who's the keeper at Rouvières. He's even older than I am. There's Panturle; there's him . . . and then there's a woman they call the Piedmontese. Just three!"

The wind stirred the sky like a sea. It made it boil and darken, then it made it foam against the mountains. The sun had disappeared. So had those still patches of peaceful azure. Nothing remained but clouds racing down towards the south.

At times the wind plunged, crushed the wood, and hurled itself on the road, weaving long tresses of dust. The horses stopped and lowered their heads. The wind passed by.

When she had recovered her breath, plump Laure asked:

"That Piedmontese, hasn't she got red hair? She always wears a big neckerchief . . . she also goes to help with the pigs. I met her while cherry-picking last year."

"You always think you know everything," Uncle Joseph replied, "and in reality you know nothing. No, she hasn't got red hair. She hardly ever leaves Aubignane. She's an old hag and very dark. 'Aunt Mamèche', that's her name. She's been up there for at least forty years. I can still remember when she arrived. She couldn't speak a word of French. She used to sit and sing at the edge of a bank. Then her husband died. Then her child died . . . . It's rather a curious story . . . ."

The wind howled behind the clouds.

"Her husband was a well-sinker. He had taken over the work for the village. Fate's an extraordinary thing! We were sinking a well at Aubignane. He was on the other side of his Alps and as likely as not out of harm's way. With that well of ours we struck on a difficult patch with a whole lot of shifting sand, and the stone mason who came from Corbières said to us: 'I'm not going down there again; I don't want to stick there.' Just at that moment the Italian turned up at Aubignane with hardly a sou in his pocket and his wife expecting a baby. God knows what made him come from over there! Fate!

"'I'll go down,' he said.

"He dug at least another four metres. He came up every evening all white and sticky, like a worm, with his hair full of sand. Then, one evening about six o'clock, all of a sudden there was a noise down below like the cracking of a nut between your teeth. We heard sand slipping and stones falling. He didn't shout. He never came up again. It was impossible to get him out. When we let down a lantern on a rope in the middle of the night, all we could see was water rising quickly above the place where the ground gave way. We had to pull up the rope as it rose. There was at least ten metres of water on top of him."

"My God!" said Michel, stopping aghast in the middle of the

road. Then he started to walk again because his coach and the others continued to move on.

"What's more," Uncle Joseph resumed, "things didn't stop there. That woman was marked out! Well, then, her husband died as I told you, and we in the village arranged to help her a bit. And we abandoned the well. We didn't want to drink that water.

"She had her child about two months afterwards. We said at the time: 'With all that she's gone through, it'll be still-born.' But it turned out to be a fine boy. Then she gradually revived. She made baskets. She used to go down to the stream. She cut the osiers and plaited them. She carried the little fellow in a bag, and while she worked she put him on the grass and sang. He used to remain quiet. It happened I don't know how many times. She gave him flowers to play with. She ought to have been careful about that. At the time he was three years old. He used to run about alone."

This time it was the uncle who stopped in the middle of the road.

"You know, it's not easy to talk going uphill! I'm out of breath. I'm getting old."

He moved on again slowly and continued with his story:

"Well, then, once during the olive season we heard something at the bottom of the valley like the howling when wolves are about. And it dried us all up with fear as we stood on our ladders. It was down below, near the stream. We remained a long time like that, then we plucked up courage. We went down through the orchards without saying a word, just wondering. Our wives remained up above, all huddled together. And the howling went on down below, enough to tear your guts.

"She was like an animal, just like an animal she was, lying on her boy. We thought that she had gone mad. Onésime Bus put his hand on her to lift her up, but she turned around on him and bit him properly.

"Finally we carried her away. Her little boy was there in the grass, already black all over and quite cold.

"His eyes were as big as your fists and his mouth was filled with a thick sort of slaver something like honey.

"He had been dead a long time. We knew that he had eaten

hemlock, because he still had bits of it in his little hand. He had found a tuft that was still green. He'd been playing with it not far from where his mother was singing."

"Good God!" groaned Mademoiselle Delphine.

All four walked for a time without uttering a word. The wind scattered the sound of the horses' bells like drops of water. The right side of the wood all of a sudden seemed to have collapsed. A small valley appeared. A path opened out onto the road. It must have climbed through the woods and wound its way to get there. It was dead. It was all green with grass. It could be seen lying there, motionless, beneath the oaks. Leaves had stuck to it and the grass had grown out of it as though it had been a dead snake.

Through the cleft in the valley one could see in the distance a landscape which was russet all over like a fox.

"That's the way over there to Aubignane," said Michel. "It doesn't seem much used. Now, good people, take your seats; and you, Uncle, squeeze up next to the girls and you'll keep warm."

Mademoiselle Delphine had big calves which overbrimmed from the tops of her high shoes in rolls of fat. When she stepped onto the running board, she knew that Michel was looking at them. She stopped, after raising one leg, and asked:

"So you say that Aubignane's over there, that place which looks so dead-alive?"

II

AUBIGNANE, LIKE A SMALL WASPS' NEST, WAS STUCK against the salient of the plateau. It was true that only three persons remained there. A grassless slope went down from the village. Almost at the bottom, there was a patch of soft earth and the wiry hair of a stunted osier bed. Below was a narrow valley with a little water. Houses were really built up there, as if balancing just on the edge of the hill. Just when the village seemed to be slipping down, the belfry was stuck in like a prop and kept it pinned up there. Not the lot: one house looked as if it had got unstuck, had slid right down to the bottom, and come to a standstill, propping itself up on its four paws at the edge of the stream, against a cypress, at the fork of the stream and what people called the road.

It was Panturle's house.

Panturle was a huge man. He looked like a piece of wood walking along. During the heat of the summer, when he had made himself a sort of sun-curtain out of fig leaves and held himself erect with his hands full of grass, he was just like a tree. His shirt hung in tatters like bark. He had a thick deformed lip like a red pimento. He moved his hand slowly towards everything he wanted to take. Generally, what he wanted did not move or had stopped moving. It was either fruit, grass, or a dead animal. He took his time. And once he grasped, he grasped well.

When he met a living animal, he looked at it without moving: it was a fox, a hare, or a big snake in the rubble. He did not move; he took his time. He knew that somewhere in a bush there was a wire noose which strangled necks that passed by.

He had a failing, if it could be called one: he talked to himself. He had started doing so immediately after his mother's death. Big as he was, he had a mother like a grasshopper. She died from the "evil", or the "vapours", as the disease was called there. It attacked old people. They had the "three sweats", the "stitch in the side", and then all the entrails would be eaten up by the disease and they died. It was the blood that curdled like milk.

When she was dead, he put her on his back and carried her to the stream. A meadow lies there, the only one in the whole countryside, a small, natural field. He left his mother there on the grass. He first took off her dress, her skirt and kerchiefs, because she had died in her clothes. He had not dared to touch her when she was suffering and screaming. But now he undressed her. She was as yellow as old tallow, yellow and dirty. That was why he did it.

He had brought a piece of velvet and half a cake of soap, and he washed his mother thoroughly from head to foot, carefully cleaning round the bones because she was thin. Then he placed her in a sheet and buried her; it was from that very evening that he started talking to himself.

Sometimes he went up to the village to see Gaubert or Aunt Mamèche.

Gaubert was a little man and all moustache. In the old days when the place was alive, when it was fully inhabited, when there were forests, olive groves, and tilled land, he was a cartwright. He made the carts, hooped the wheels, and shod the mules. At that time, he had a fine black moustache. He also had hard muscles, as firm as bamboo, and too strong for his small body. They sent him bounding across the forge, hither and thither, back and forth, always moving and springing, like a rat. This was why he got the name of "wagtail", that little bird which the bushes throw to one another unceasingly like a ball for three seasons of the year.

It was Gaubert who made the finest ploughs. He had a secret charm. He had dug a hole under a cypress, and the hole had filled with water, and the water was bitter as sheep-gall, probably because it seeped up between the cypress roots. When he wanted to make a plough, he took a big piece of ash and put it to soak in the hole. He left it for a fairly long time, day and night, and sometimes would come and look at it as he smoked his pipe. He turned it, ran his fingers over it, replaced it in the water, let it get well soaked, and washed it with his hands. Sometimes he would watch it without doing anything. The sun, like some bright object, swam around the piece of wood. When Gaubert went back to the forge, the knees of his trousers were all green with crushed grass. Finally, once the beam was ready, he carried it back on his shoulder, all dripping with water as if he had just brought it up from the sea. Then he would sit down in front of his forge. He placed the piece of wood on his thigh. He put a little pressure on it at either end. He twisted it gently and the wood took the form of his thigh. In this way he produced as fine a plough as any you could find on the furrows. Once it was ready, people would come and look at it, discuss it, and someone would say:

"Gaubert, how much do you want for it?"

Then he would stop jumping from the anvil to the tub and say: "Already promised."

Nowadays little Gaubert seemed more than ever to be all moustache. His muscles had eaten him up. They had left nothing but bone and skin which had become as hard as a drum-head. But he had worked too much, and even more with his heart than with his arms. It had now grown into a sort of madness.

His forge was at the top of the village. It was cold and dead. His chimney had fought with the wind and his fireplace had become littered with broken bricks and plaster. Rats had eaten the leather of the bellows. That is where old Gaubert lived. He had made his bed next to the iron which remained to be forged but had not been forged. It lay there frozen, in the shadows under the dust. At night, he lay beside it. On the floor of beaten earth the damp had forced up big swellings. But the anvil was still there, and around it, like a lump of hardened skin, was a clear piece of floor tanned by the smith's feet. The anvil was bright, alive and clear, ready to sing. A hammer was also resting against it to deliver the blows. The wood of its handle shone with the same friendly appearance as the anvil. Whenever Gaubert felt bored, he took hold of the hammer with both hands, raised it, and struck the anvil. He went on like that, for no purpose, just for the sound, to hear the sound. His life was in each of those strokes. The sound of the anvil echoed through the countryside and sometimes came upon Panturle while he was hunting. After all, he could still have a talk with that.

Everything was frozen up and silent that morning. Even the wind was silent, but not really dead. It waved about a little and beat its tail gently against the hard sky. There was no sun yet. The sky was empty. It was all frozen up, like a sheet hanging out in the frost.

Panturle had already lit the fire. He had got up in the white of dawn. He stood there in front of the hearth, watching the wild flames galloping over the dry olive branches. He hung up the cauldron of potatoes. Water and potatoes were at one and the same time soup, stew, and bread for him.

Olive-wood fires are good because they catch quickly, but they are just like colts, prancing around elegantly without thinking of work. When the frisky flame reared against the cauldron, Panturle checked it by hitting the embers with the palm of his hand, which was as hard as old bacon rind.

Holding his hand up for a last stroke, he said to the fire: "Will you keep quiet?"

It began to keep quiet. It had had enough of being beaten. It rubbed its long, red hairs against the rump of the cauldron.

Suddenly the wind roared more loudly than the fire, and the sun rose.

A shepherd's long whistle came down from the village. It seemed to have been aimed like an arrow, straight at Panturle's house. It could be felt. It went right through the walls and tingled against the cauldron on the fire.

Panturle let go the branch with which he was stirring his soup. He placed his two big fingers under his tongue and, getting red as a tomato, replied with the same kind of whistle which went up the hill.

This was a habit. He knew that Gaubert had reached the church square and had wished him good-day in his own manner, with his old tongue and his old fingers.

But that morning it was earlier than usual and seemed to mean: "Come along!"

He did not think that it was because of something that had gone wrong. It seemed to be a pretty healthy whistle. Besides, it did not say hurriedly: "Come, quick, quick, quick!"

No, it said merely: "Come along!" as if meaning: "You might just come and see."

He would go and see. First he fed the goat. She was loose and all alone in the big black stables. She bounded at once towards the open door. He watched her eating. As she shuffled among the fodder, he touched her head and said: "Come on now. We're going up to Gaubert."

When approaching that side of Aubignane, hanging above the valley on the right, one comes straight upon Mamèche's house. It was not her property, of course, but nobody would come and claim it from her. She had only to choose among the heap of broken-down houses, and find one with as much roof as possible.

Panturle went slightly out of his way to reach her door, and said:

"Here's Caroline, Mamèche. Take the milk."

As the goat on the threshold started trembling with her voice and hair, Mamèche called out in Italian:

"*Cabro, cabro!*"

The goat replied and went in.

Gaubert waited in front of his forge.

"So, you've put on your best jacket?" Panturle asked.

It was true. He had put on his best jacket, and his best hat, and his best corduroy trousers.

"I'm leaving," said Gaubert gently.

A big travelling trunk with iron hoops crushed the grass on the road.

"I'm going away," he said; "my son sent word yesterday evening through the shepherd from Pamponnets. He says he's anxious about leaving me alone this winter.

"He says it'll be better for me over there. He says they've prepared the room next to the kitchen for me because of the stove. He says that I'll be glad to be with Belline and the little ones, and that Belline will look after me well. I'm eighty."

Panturle looked at Gaubert, spick and span, and at the trunk ready for the departure. He noticed also in the middle of the forge a big parcel all done up in a sheet knotted at the corners.

"My boy let me know that he would come with the horse as far as Font-de-la-Reine-Porque," Gaubert said. "He can't go further. They say our road has crashed down into the ravine."

"I can just get by on foot," Panturle said.

"That's really what I whistled to you for," Gaubert replied.

He showed him the parcels.

"It's no good trying with the big box," Panturle said. "It wouldn't get by. D'you particularly want it?"

"No," Gaubert said. "They're things of my wife's time."

"And that, in there?" Panturle asked.

"Ah, my poor fellow! . . ." Gaubert sighed. "Come and have a look."

Old Gaubert undid the parcel in the forge. His hands trembled. There, lying in the sheet, was his anvil.

"I'd somehow like to take that, you know," he said.

Panturle understood. One has got to understand that sort of thing.

"We'll try," he said. "And Joseph, when's he expecting you?"

"He sent word that he'd leave home at sunrise," Gaubert replied.

"Are you quite ready?" Panturle asked.

"Yes."

"So you were moping . . . ?"

15

Panturle had asked the question without malice. He said just what came into his head without meaning to be unpleasant to Gaubert. But Gaubert bowed his head in silence.

It was hard work, especially through the Bergerie wood. There was no longer a road. Panturle first took Gaubert up, giving him a hand, and then went down again to fetch the anvil.

Gaubert looked down from above and said to him:

"There, catch hold of the thyme on the right. Put your foot on the stone there, on the left. Don't catch hold of that grass. It's dead. That's it! Ah, my poor fellow!"

Panturle laboured up the rubble with the anvil on the thick part of his shoulder. From time to time he let out a "God Almighty!" which pushed him along for a good metre.

When he reached the top he threw the anvil into the dead leaves, took a few good breaths of cold air, rubbed his eye, into which the sweat had dripped, and began to laugh.

"We managed her after all, the bitch!" he exclaimed.

Gaubert laughed too. He felt warm with pleasure at the thought that the worst bit was over. He opened the parcel slightly to have a look at the anvil. There it was, dead to all that was happening.

"She little knows what trouble she's giving," he said.

Then Panturle started to think aloud again:

"So the boy really wants you?" he said. "Or did you perhaps complain? Do you think that you'll get used to living away from Aubignane? You were born at Aubignane, weren't you? But perhaps he needed you over there? So you'll be next to the kitchen? I wonder if Belline won't mind."

Gaubert replied by nodding or shaking his head without speaking.

The village was now out of sight. All that could be seen was the brow of a wooded hill ruffled by the wind.

When Joseph saw them approaching he cried:

"Hey there! Make haste," for it was cold around Reine-Porque.

"There!" said Panturle, setting down the anvil.

"What's that?" asked Joseph. He looked inside the parcel. One never knows with old men. Sometimes they have hiding places where they stow away their money. There have even been some who amassed ten kilos like that. When he saw that it was the anvil, he exclaimed: "You're mad, Father!"

It was Panturle who replied: "No, leave him alone. It's because you don't know."

When old Gaubert had sat down in the cart, Panturle placed the anvil between his legs. Gaubert thanked him, his son applied the whip, and they were off.

Panturle watched them. Gaubert had placed his hands on the anvil. It was there between his legs. He was stroking it and he was happy. It would have been worse than death for him to have left it behind.

The water of the spring at Font-de-la-Reine-Porque was already frozen over. The spring appeared to be lost and miserable, abandoned there, unprotected, in the middle of the open fields. It had been made with a tube of cane and the hollow trunk of a poplar tree. There it remained, all alone. In summer the sun, drinking like a donkey, dried up its basin in a few gulps. The wind washed up the water from under the spout and frittered it away in the dust. In winter the spring froze to the very core. It was unlucky. So was the rest of the land.

Away in the distance a "Ho!" and the sound of a whip could still be heard. Joseph's cart was already at the top of the black earth. Then they must have passed over the col, for the sounds ceased. Suddenly Panturle felt frozen to the marrow. He started running towards the village. As he ran he shouted: "Hey, hey . . . " That was company.

"Oho, Mamèche!"

"Oho, my boy!"

Mamèche's voice was grave and hard. It came from deep down.

"Is Caroline done?" Panturle asked.

"She's done," Mamèche answered. "It's boiling and ready for you, if you come in."

"*La saluta*," said Panturle, pushing open the door.

About as much daylight as a layer of straw in stables covered the flagstones. It did not go up to the ceiling because the upper panes of the windows had been replaced by boards. They were old windows and even with the two bottom panes, which were still of glass, one had to be careful. One of them was starting to get unstuck, and nothing hindered the wind from blowing through the crack. Thus the light shone only on the lower half of the people in the room. Daylight covered Mamèche's body from her bare feet up to her waist.

Near the table there was a big Holy Virgin of plaster, with the light shining on her. Mamèche had taken her home with her when the church had become to all intents and purposes a wolves' lair overrun with grass.

The Virgin seemed to be quite at home with her bare feet, her rosary of olive stones, and her sky-blue, stiff dress.

What could be seen of Mamèche was much the same but all black.

Three bowls of hot milk steamed on the hearthstone.

"No more need to put three there," Panturle said as he sat down by the firewood.

"What? Is he . . . ?"

"No, he has just gone away."

She lowered her face towards Panturle. It was thin and rusted, like the blade of an old axe. All that was alive was in the fire of her eyes.

"What was that?"

"I said he's just gone away."

"But where?"

Caught in the sunlight, Mamèche's lips, after pronouncing the words, went on moving in their eagerness to speak.

"To his boy," Panturle replied.

"To his boy? . . . To his boy?" Mamèche drew herself up. She walked one step and then another towards the door. Panturle looked at her face up there in the dark to which his eyes were gradually growing accustomed. Her long toe-nails, like claws, scratched the stone.

"Ah, Madonna!" she cried out suddenly, and her whole throat contracted.

She fell down in a heap and remained there, wringing her hands and swaying her head as if in the wind.

"Madonna, Madonna! So they're all gone, all of them . . . . And I, am I not old too? Do I go off? Have I got a child to go to? What use has my dead man been in your swine of a country? What was the good of his going and looking for water for you all? He threw his life away looking for it. That's what he did. And I, would I go off? Am I not old too? Ah, porca!"

She snatched up the bowl of hot milk prepared for Gaubert. She threw the milk in the Virgin's face. A veil of steam flowed down the straight folds of the blue dress and then evaporated. The wet rosary shone. The Virgin smiled with the skin of the milk on her lips.

Mamèche threatened her with her hairy black fist, which looked like a frozen quince.

"*Porca!* To think that you can do as you please, and that you beat me like wheat and dried me like wheat and are eating me up like wheat . . . . So you let my prayers rot, did you!" she continued. "You may well look at me with your chalk eyes. Do I look at you like that? I'll tell you straight, I will, and what else can you do to me anyhow? You've bled me dry already!"

"Listen to me," said Panturle gently.

"No! I've had enough. Isn't it true what I say, now tell me, you, Braë! You know that my man is deep down there in your earth, that he went down to the bottom over there to suck up the water with his mouth, right to the very veins of the source. And just for you to drink, for your soup. You know that's true, Braë. Do you think that I wasn't made just like other women, with breasts and a belly, with a mouth and lips to kiss him, to keep him and to please him! He's down below, stark dead with his mouth full of your earth! Look at her there, laughing away! What did she do that day? Who was she abed with that day? . . . And what good did his death do? When they'd made him die, they just started going off, one after the other, like pigs after acorns . . . . And I'd like to know what she's done to keep them here – look at her, going on laughing away there!

Ah, Holy Virgin, if you're there to be like a big bug sucking at my blood, then I'm done with you!"

"Now listen," said Panturle gently, "Listen, Mamèche, come here by me, come. The two of us are still here . . . ."

Mamèche dragged herself on her knees up to Panturle. She leaned up against the man, feeling him with her long, bony fingers:

"Ah, Braë," she sighed, "tongues are thick!"

They remained like that for some time without speaking.

"Son!" the woman said.

"Mother!" Panturle replied.

Because suddenly in that silence which they had shared, he thought of his mother who was dead too, and eaten up by the osiers down there . . . .

Leaning against the man, Mamèche had a nervous trembling, like that of a goat. She quieted down. She stroked his big, solid thighs and then spoke gentle words coming straight from her heart, which had become soft as a fig.

"I'm thinking of my child, my little one, my Rolando, who's under the roots of the grass," she said. "It's not justice, Braë! Those others have still got them in the flesh walking about, yet they've gone off to look for a better place. But for me, all that was dear to me has become the grass and water of this place, and I'll stay here until I become part of this earth as well."

"So will I, Mamèche," said Panturle. "I've got Mother . . . "

"I'll tell you, my boy, the thing that's digging into me like a spade and making me suffer like a martyr. As long as we're here it's all right, but after that it'll become wild woods and be all overgrown . . . . Listen. Just after I married my man we worked near Pignatello. I used to go with him on the road. We went through the woods and there were charcoal burners there. One day we approached a place where a heap of charcoal was always smoking. The grass had been removed right round it. We knew that the man was going to cut the wood and that he'd bring it to that very spot. We wanted to know why. We went nearer and saw a sort of hut there, *una cosa di niente*, a bit of a thing, you could have put it into a nutshell. There was a woman in front of it and two children sprawling around like young dogs. We asked our question and the woman told us the reason. Those two twins weren't the only children. Another one was in the earth, and there'd be no more pranks with him. They'd placed a wooden fence round the spot. The woman's father was also below the ground – a very old man – and a baby girl was there too, born dead. But above all, Braë, there was the man who kept on going through the smoke of the charcoal kiln. He was alive, right enough, and inside him who knows how many children there were, ready to come? . . . Perhaps it's made a village since then . . . . But here . . . "

"You must drink, Mamèche," said Panturle, and he took a bowl. The milk had become cold. It seemed to have frozen under a layer of thick skin. Before drinking, Mamèche put her black finger into the milk and drew out a goat's hair with her nail.

"I'm going down," Panturle said. "Where have you put Caroline?"

"Behind there, in the pasture."

"Have you still got potatoes?"

"Yes."

"Try and make them last till it gets really cold. Then I'll go and look up the man at Bourettes to see if he'll give me some more in exchange for a hare. Have you all you need?"

"Yes, son. We'll have to stick together now to hold on here."

Standing in front of the door, Panturle called the goat. She came and the pebbles on the path could be heard rolling under Panturle's heavy tread.

Mamèche then remained alone in front of the Virgin, who continued to laugh under the skin of milk.

"*Bellissima!*" she cried.

She opened out her long black arms.

"*Mia bella*, whom I love more than anything, let me wipe you."

She took the Virgin on her knees. She undid the rosary and wiped the olive stones one by one. She spat on the corner of her skirt and washed the Virgin's mouth.

"There now, don't worry, you're still my lovely one."

Then she looked into the far end of the room at something which was her sorrow and her memories.

Panturle came back to Mamèche. It was four o'clock. It was the moment when at that season the sun caught onto the pine up there and clung to it a little before falling behind the hills.

The whole day Panturle had continued to carry the anvil on his shoulders – an anvil of air which was imaginary but much heavier than the real one of that morning.

The whole day long!

From time to time he felt the little bruise which the corner of the iron had made on his shoulder. He kept on saying to himself: "Gaubert's gone!" That meant that he was alone now at Aubignane, alone with Mamèche, who was not much of a distraction. Oh, no! To think that he would no longer hear the heart of the village beat. The anvil had gone. It had gone away on Joseph's cart, between Gaubert's legs. He would no longer hear: "Bang, bang; bang, bang; bang, bang," which till then had been a living noise in the village. It used to tell him in the heart of the wood: "Gaubert's bored. Gaubert's thinking of the time when he was master of the ploughs."

And the whole day he continued to carry the heavy anvil. He was still carrying it when he went up to see Mamèche.

The sun's last finger let go of the pine up there. The sun fell behind the hills. A few drops of blood splashed the sky. Night washed them out with her grey hand.

A fire was burning on the hearth, but the wind had choked up the chimney and it blew its music with smoke and flying cinders, flattening out the flames.

Panturle chewed his quid of tobacco – a bit of weed mixed with wisps of grass and animal hairs which he scraped together from the bottom of his pocket.

It was bitter.

"Blast this weather!" he said.

The wind had blown up for a three days' storm.

"Turn round and let me look at you a bit," Mamèche said. "Place yourself in front of the fire a little, Braë, and let me have a look."

"What do you want?" Panturle asked.

"There now, turn a bit," she said.

Panturle bent down and placed himself in the firelight.

He was still a young man. He had blood in his cheeks, and bright eyes. He had a good beard on his face: goód, healthy hair, well fed with blood. He had a fine layer of flesh on his bones – the firm flesh of a man matured by forty years of life. His hands were strong. The strength flowed like oil right to his finger-tips.

"Have you had a good look?" he asked.

"Yes."

"Well?"

"I'm thinking of that charcoal burner."

"Yes," said Panturle.

He spat in the embers and continued: "Yes, there ought to be a woman. I have a longing sometimes on fine days. But where's the woman who'd come here?"

"Where is she? She's everywhere if you force her."

"Oh, so you think it's done like that, do you?"

"Don't you count, then?"

"I'm like the others, but I tell you it's not done that way. It's got to come from further off and from a long time ago."

"If I brought one to you, would you take her?"

Panturle stopped chewing his quid. He looked into the depths of Mamèche's eyes and considered. He remained like that, silent and motionless, with a pondering look. She repeated:

"If I brought you one, would you take the woman?"

He assented gravely, bending half his body, and said: "Yes, I'd take her!"

Winter was hard that year. Never had such thick ice been seen on the stream. Never had the cold been so biting. It was so bitter that it froze up the wind in the depths of the sky. The countryside shivered in silence. The moor which stretched out above the village was all frozen. There was not a cloud in the sky. Every morning a russet sun rose in silence. With a few indifferent paces it strode across the whole breadth of the sky and day was over. Night heaped up the stars like grain.

Panturle had taken on his real winter appearance. The hair on his cheeks had grown longer and had tangled like the fleece of a sheep.

He was a bush. Before eating, he had to brush his beard from his mouth. He had become more savage too. He no longer talked to his tools. He had bound his feet and legs in cloths and had attached them with string. Like that he was warm, did not slip, and made no noise. He always went about with his knife and his cunning wire. He hunted. He needed meat.

Mamèche also hunted in her own way. She went in for small game: sparrows tamed by the cold and all fluffed up like balls of wool. She did what people in those parts call "embalming grain". She boiled some old oats with some rue leaves and thorn-apple and then strewed the mixture in front of her door. The sparrows ate it and died on the spot. Before cooking them she removed their gizzards, cut them open with old scissors, and emptied out the grain onto a paper to use it again.

Naturally Panturle did not forget her. He brought big pieces of hare, gave her some thrushes, and sometimes whole small rabbits. For he himself had plenty. He ate as much as he wanted and put some by in his cellar to exchange it later for potatoes with that old lunatic at Bourettes.

Winter continued to hold all in its grip and the days succeeded one another without change.

Panturle was at Vincent's wood. He had placed some hare springes and was watching.

In the distance he saw Mamèche. She was also out. She had gone up to the moor. She was standing erect like a tree-trunk. He was going to call when he realized that she was speaking. He listened.

She was saying: "It must first come from you if it is to last."

She was speaking to something there in front of her, yet there was nothing in front of her but the moor, blighted by disease and cold.

It happened again a second time but not in the same place; as if she were visiting all her friends to ask them a favour. That time it was on Resplandin hill, in the very middle of the thicket.

Panturle approached quietly on his cloth-covered feet. He approached her as if he wanted to catch her in his snare. She remained in front of that dirty bit of hill, bespattered with frozen

24

mud and hoar frost under wretched, bare trees. And she was saying: "Don't bother about that. It's my affair. I'll go and fetch her wherever she happens to be, but I tell you, it must first come from you."

She was certainly speaking to all that in front of her, because when she had finished she moved her arm and pointed her finger at the grass, the tree, and the ground.

Little by little the time came when the winter, like bad fruit, softened. Up to a certain moment it had remained hard, green, and very acid. Then suddenly it became tender. The air was almost warm. There was no wind yet. For the past three days a big cloud had been dancing in the same place, anchored to the southern horizon.

And today there had been rain. Like a bird it arrived, settled, and went away. The shadow of its wings had been seen passing over the hills of Névières. It came back and hovered around Aubignane, then flew off towards the plains. After that the sun came out and, like a mouth, breathed warmth.

Panturle had undone his cloth leggings and placed himself in the sun. He had stretched out his bare feet in the warmth and was amusing himself by wiggling his toes. Caroline looked at him, disconcerted.

Mamèche turned towards the south and for a long time watched the motionless cloud. She sniffed up long breaths of air, tasting it as one samples a wine to see if it is ready, if it has finished fermenting, and if it has sufficient alcohol. And then, behold: the cloud went up slowly towards the open sky. It left the coast and set out on its voyage. That is what she wanted to see.

Then she went home. She boiled some potatoes, taking old ones, big ones, of all sorts. When they were boiled she lined them up on the table, counted them, and started calculating on her fingers.

"One day, two days, perhaps three, perhaps four." Finally she said: "The reckoning's right."

She put the potatoes in a napkin with a handful of salt and did up the bundle with a clematis stem. After that she removed the rosary from the Virgin's neck and put it on her own. She lingered awhile, looking at the Virgin. Her lips did not move.

Then the travelling cloud passed in front of the window. It had gained speed and was ascending to the north.

That same night there was a great upheaval in the sky. All that the cold had frozen and hardened, all that it had held immovable, all this was suddenly delivered and started living again. The clouds belched forth rain, the wind blew up from the four corners of the earth, and the withered leaves on the trees burst into song. The obstinate oaks, which had kept their fleece of the previous year, chattered in the wind with the voice of the torrent.

Until sunset the upheaval went on. Then Panturle shut up Caroline, who seemed a bit excited. He looked up towards the village. Mamèche was up there sitting on the rampart and looking at something in the sky towards the south.

The night came, as thick as pea soup. But all the same it was more pleasant than the nights which seemed like blades on the grindstone, with their bunches of stars. It was more pleasant firstly because it was more caressing and its skin was softer. Besides, it was penetrated by the voice of the stream, by the voice of the cypress, and once by something that might have been the bark of a fox if the time of year had not been so early.

Panturle went to sleep quickly. He felt limp without knowing why, for he had not hunted for several days. He was not limp from tiredness. He felt limp, as if holes had been made in his arms, holes had been made in his legs, and all his strength had been drained. Yes, and as if the strength had been replaced by milk of savory flowers. He felt that it was flowing all over his body. It tickled him and made him laugh. But he was limp and soon fell asleep.

He was roused from his sleep – it must have been midnight or more – by a loud cry that hit him in the ear like a stone.

"It's Mamèche!"

Without even seeing the door, he took two bounds and was outside. His eyes were still heavy with sleep.

It was Mamèche, right enough. She was up there on the village wall with a torch in her hand. She raised her hand with the flame. One could make out her whole figure. She had put her black shawl on her head. The smoke from the fire rose towards the north.

"What's the matter?" Panturle cried with all his strength.

"Nothing."

"Sick?"

"No."

"Well, then . . . ?"

For a moment she made no reply. She appeared to be gathering her strength to shout loud enough to make herself understood. Then, pointing to the south with her torch, she cried: "It's coming, it's coming!"

"She must have gone a bit mad," Panturle said to himself.

All the same, he also turned towards the south. Something had changed since nightfall. A lissom and sweet-smelling force had darted out into the night. It gave the impression of a well-rested young animal. It was warm, just like the life under an animal's fur, and it smelt bitter. Panturle sniffed the air. Something like hawthorn. As it leapt forward, the whole earth seemed to be talking about it.

The wind of spring!

The next morning Panturle opened his door on a delivered world. Life had returned, life abounding with action and swift movement. The whole wood, with its arms aloft, joined on the spot in a great dance of excitement. Big shadow-ships floated over the hills. The clouds in their flight bounded from one shore of the sky to the other. A crow passed by all aflutter, blown over and over by the wind, like a dead leaf.

Panturle let Caroline loose. Ah! She was away at once. She might have been a jet of water. She went off capering. She seemed like a wave of fur over the grass. She planted herself on her four paws in front of the cypress and threatened it with her horns for a moment, then went off suddenly in the opposite direction with the grass whistling against her legs.

"That's perhaps what Mamèche meant," Panturle said to himself. "But anyhow, what does it matter? Spring is here, right enough. That's clear."

Nevertheless he went up to see for himself.

There was nobody at Mamèche's house. Her room was empty. Her mattress had been rolled up. The table and chairs had been lined up against the wall as if they were to be left for a long time. An unused sheet had been placed on the table. It had been folded eight times and rested there conspicuously. Panturle knew the sheet well. Everybody knew it well. It was the sheet that all old women keep unused at the bottom of their cupboards for the time when they will be enveloped in it at the end.

Panturle went back to the doorstep and cried: "Ho, Mamèche!"

He searched the entire village, crying thus till midday.

He entered all the houses and looked under the ruins of all the walls blown over by the last wind.

"Mamèche! Ho, Mamèche!"

Then he went back to the house which was still empty, with the unused sheet on the table. He said to himself: "I'll go and have a look on the plateau."

And he went onto the plateau.

One went rarely onto the plateau and never willingly. It was a completely flat stretch of land extending until it was out of sight. Grass, grass, grass, without a tree. And flat. When a man walked up there, he alone topped the grass. It made a curious impression. One felt marked out for a sudden blast of wind or some other bad turn. The plateau began at the last houses at the top of Aubignane and went on indefinitely. In reality it went on as far as Blaine, forty-two kilometres away as the crow flies, but one did not necessarily know that. Besides, as a rule it gave the impression that it was not going towards anything human. Over there, in the distance, a grey barrier of dust appeared above it, scurrying before the wind.

There was nothing on the plateau: only the wind. And the same wind that had appeared on the previous night: the goat-wind of spring. There it was, up yonder. There it was, over there with its dust. Now it was here. There it was again over there in the grass. It was everywhere.

"Mamèche, Mamèche!"

Nothing. The wind came to see what was the matter and then went away again.

Panturle's throat was hoarse from shouting so much.

"What can have been the matter with the woman? Who'd have said that she, too, would go away like that?"

He returned to the village. It was evening. At Mamèche's house the little day that remained lighted up the white sheet on the table. Panturle pulled the door to, then went to the rampart and scanned the whole countryside to its very depths: the flock of hills and the long, grey, flat line which was the border of the plateau. His eyes went from the right edge to the left edge.

Behind him was Aubignane, empty.

He again searched the whole countryside right to its depths, and then he said aloud:

"There! Now I am alone."

III

GÉDÉMUS, THE KNIFE-GRINDER, WALKED OUT OF THE tobacco shop at Sault. He had just bought six packs of tobacco. He held them against his breast as he closed the door.

"You're afraid the price will go up, taking in stock like that?" cried Reboulin from the other side of the street.

"Fool!" said Gédémus. "When you want a smoke, you've just got to take three steps and you're at the shop; but I'm leaving tomorrow. Can't you see it's spring? I'll be four days without being able to buy tobacco."

He put the packs in his pockets, keeping one in his hand. He opened it and began to roll a cigarette as he walked across the street.

"You might let me have a bit," said Reboulin. "I've left mine on the mantelpiece."

"Go easy then; it must last me a week."

"Does it take you a week to get over there?"

"Don't be ridiculous; only four days. But when you're on the other side it's not yet the tobacco shop, you know."

"D'you sleep on the plateau?"

"Yes."

"And you don't mind?"

"No."

"It's true that your cart's full of sharp knives, so you don't risk much."

"Oh, that wouldn't be much good, but I've got to go that way. I won't say I enjoy it much, but I've never been much afraid. What matters is to know your bearings all right, and to go by good stages. From this place I'll be going as far as La Trinité. I'll spend the night there in a good, sound barn. The next day I'll go as far as the Crow's sheepfold. From the sheepfold onwards it's more difficult. The path has disappeared and you must know your way about and never lose your head. Further on, I turn right: two or three hours' walk, and I reach the Gallibert farm."

"Are you taking Arsule along with you?"

"D'you expect me to leave her?"

"No. I was only asking. You're a rascal, Gédémus. You can no longer do without that woman."

"Ah, what an idea of yours! At my age ... why, you'll have forgotten that yourself before it comes back to me. Can't you see I make her draw my cart?"

Arsule?

Ah, it's a long story.

Arsule first went by the name of "Mademoiselle Irène", and even "Mademoiselle Irène of the Big Theatres of Paris and of the World". That, of course, was all a lie. Yet it was written by hand on a poster stuck on the window of the Café des Deux Mondes.

In point of fact, the poor girl had arrived by the Montbrun road, behind a cart covered over with dirty old sheets. A man, who looked like a murderer, led the mule by the muzzle. He was down on the poster as "The Famous Tony in His Repertoire". For the time being his repertoire consisted only of foul words. He shouted at his jade of a mule, stuck there on all fours in the shade of the washing-shed.

Mademoiselle Irène stood behind the cart. She was tired out

from walking along the road in an old pair of men's buttoned shoes which were too large for her feet, and let herself be dragged along by holding onto the brake-rope. She was powdered with dust up to her waist.

At the Café des Deux Mondes they had put up a stage with six marble-topped tables in the corner where the old billiard table used to stand which they had since burnt. In the evening the place was so full that the audience overflowed into the kitchen. Mother Alloison no longer knew which way to turn. Everybody was rapping for a drink: "A coffee, here! A coffee!" And there she stood, saying: "Well, make room for me to get at my coffee-pot."

The people just laughed and it made no difference. They went on rapping for nothing. Finally things improved a bit. Everybody did his best to help her, and when it was something like quiet, Mademoiselle Irène got onto the stage. She had poor, scullery-maid's hands. Her eyes had something about them that made you sorry for her. There she stood, completely tired out. She was there to sing, and you could see that her mind was full of the pangs of the long trudge and of a thousand things that were obviously far more painful than the road for a woman. There she stood.

It made the people laugh.

That put her out completely.

It ended in a fight. Tony "in his repertoire" wanted to smash a bottle over her head, but the people would not stand for that. Finally there was a free-for-all. Women screamed and glasses were broken. But the boys of Sault were not much the worse for it, because they all went for Tony together. Marguerite's son sprained his wrist a little, when he punched the marble counter by mistake.

That was all very well. But the next morning the woman did not dare to set out with Tony, and so stayed there, sitting near the fountain, all alone, her face besmirched with tears. She was no longer crying. You could not tell whether she was thinking of anything or not. She was gazing at the water flowing from the fountain.

It was lavender time. At noon, all the men working for Garino, the lavender-dealer, arrived. They came down from the hills to have a rest from the scorching heat. The woman was just what they wanted. They gathered round her and began saying one thing and another to her. Finally one of them said: "Come along, we'll give you something to eat." She looked up vacantly at the man, then went with them. But instead of giving her something to eat they made her soak up wine and then raped her. They had taken her into Martel's stable, and all stood in front of the door, laughing, while one of them was inside with the girl. When the man came out he was flushed and started laughing louder than the others. But one could see that his laughter was rather forced. Then another went in. And so on.

It was fat Marie Guindon who snatched her out of their hands. She went for them one after the other. She placed her fists on her hips and gave them a piece of her mind.

"Aren't you ashamed of yourselves? You're a fine lot, indeed! Look at him, there! You could take him under your hat, like a butterfly. There's none of you who would dare to touch me! I've a mind to slap all your faces!"

Then she went to fetch Mademoiselle Irène. The poor girl was as limp as a rope and covered with straw. She said to her:

"Go into the kitchen, my girl. Get clear of them."

All that happened more than five years ago.

In the village they called her Arsule. It was easier to say than Irène and, besides, Irène is a town name and a lie. Arsule is a local name. After that she stayed with Gédémus. She made his soup for him and did everything else.

The road climbed up, and with it two rows of plane trees. The houses did not go further than the turning. There they said "Good-bye" and remained squatting on the borders of the meadows. They watched the road setting out for the open country. The plane trees went on for a while, up to the middle of the slope, but there they also stopped. Then the little road went on all alone. With a jerk of its loins it sprang up over the hillock, then good-bye for ever.

As long as they were in the shade it was not so bad, but as soon as they were in the sun Arsule knew that Gédémus would leave the strap and say:

"Catch hold of it a bit. I'll just roll myself a cigarette."

She would catch hold of it. But after that she remained at the strap as long as the work lasted. Sometimes he would help her up steep hills. Then, in October, on their way back, when they reached the first plane trees, with shade and the downward slope before them, ten minutes from the house, Gédémus would say:

"Now hand it over a bit." And he would take the strap again.

Arsule knew all that by heart. She also knew the weight of the little hand-cart. First, and above all, there was the grinding-machine with its heavy wheel of thick, rough stone and its strong wooden frame which had to be prevented from shaking when Gédémus worked the treadle and the grindstone went. It was heavy. But then, of course, it had to be. There was also a big cloak to carry, and food to last until the first farmhouse. That meant food for four days. But that was not the heavy part of it.

Then one had to pull . . . . The main thing was to get used to the work.

The wretched vegetable gardens, which had only a slight fleece of salad, spinach, or leeks, gradually receded into the background. They were all lying huddled together down there, under the shelter of the village, and some of them even found their way in amongst the houses.

On reaching the brow of the hillock they began to hear the wild purr of the juniper shrubs. It was down there, on the other side of a small vale. The earth was bare, with only an old poplar at the bottom of the fold. They climbed up the other side, along a lane which had had to be hewn out with a miner's drill. No longer any herbs except for a few lonely patches of thyme and a sage plant with the usual bee on it. The rock rumbled under their feet. They went on and then turned. No more village, no more poplars. Only ten more difficult strides, ten strides which brought every-thing into play – the shoulder that bore forward, the thigh that pushed on, the foot that acted as a spring, the head that controlled – yet another, and another . . . . Gédémus was also tugging at the cart. Ten strides and then it was too late to come back; the big juniper shrubs blocked the road behind them. They were now full in the open country. It was the plateau, the real plateau!

Flat as a threshing-floor, it was a meadow of clouds. The path was nothing more than a tiny rill, dried up to the bone.

As far as the eye could perceive, it was like a great sea, darkened by a surge of juniper shrubs. Junipers, junipers, junipers. Broad-winged, silent crows soared up from the bush and the wind carried them away.

Gédémus and Arsule walked on alone. The wind blew through the frame of the grinding-machine as across the masts of a bark.

"Haven't we gone wrong?"

"No, come on . . . . It's all right."

"What's that, over there?"

"Nothing. A tree. A dead tree."

"Are you sure?"

"Yes, come on. Each time we come here you're afraid. What do you suppose it can be? It's a tree and nothing more. Come on, I tell you."

Then, suddenly, they emerged from that sea of junipers. Just on the outskirts of the wood the great, grassy solitude began. A cloud had just alighted on the grass yonder, in the depths. It rose. They began to see a slight strip of sky between the grass and it. And thus, low as it was, it came on. It passed over, only ten metres up, unfeeling and powerful.

The shadow walked on the earth like an animal; the grass was flattened; the sandy stretches smoked. The shadow walked on its supple legs. There it was, old and heavy on one's shoulders. No sound. It went its way. It passed by. That was all.

"Don't be afraid, I tell you."

"What's that, over there?"

"Where?"

"There! Standing in the grass and all black, with arms . . . it looks like . . . "

"It's a tree again. Wait a bit . . . . I wonder if we've not gone wrong. There were not so many trees over here as that. Yet it's a dead tree, all right. What else could it be? We are certainly going in the right direction. There, on our right, are the Chenerilles sands and look, on our left over there, the long range of Lure. In front of us there's Crackskull Pass. We're all right. Come on, it's only another tree. You notice everything, too!"

Now they stood in the midst of the open country, the very midst. There was nothing more. The transparent brim of the sky rested all round on the grass.

Towards noon they stopped for a snack. Arsule shook her shoulder out of the leather strap and swung her arm two or three times to take the stiffness out of it. Gédémus recognized the place. He was glad.

"It's all right. I recognize it like a man's face." He was relieved and added: "Ah! We can rest a bit now. My head's had enough of that wind!"

They pulled out the little box from under the grindstone. First it was a big chunk of bread, as fat as a sucking-pig; then, sausage; then a thick piece of ham with a sheet of soft paper stuck on the raw of the slice. There were also tins of sardines and three heads of garlic with which Gédémus began the meal.

They were sitting in the long grass. The wind gathered speed and leapt over them. They were sheltered. All was well. On that plateau which was so flat, so extensive, and so well spread out under the sun and the wind, you could be comfortable only when seated. The warmth of the earth stole up into your loins; the grass was all round like a warm, sheltering sheepskin. When you walked, it was just the opposite: you felt naked and weak. It seemed as if, over that great stretch, everywhere eyes were watching you and things spying on you. But when sitting you were comfortable. You could think of something else; you were not all the time obliged to think of that flat ground and of the wind whetting its teeth upon it.

Arsule also ate garlic. Her head overtopped the grass; she looked at the great plateau which lay under the sky like another sky upside down. She looked at a mountain beyond, which was as blue as deep water, and at the tall grass galloping away into the unknown. She looked and then suddenly she said: "Oh! Oh!" twice, and remained like that with her mouth open and full of bread and garlic.

"What?"

Arsule's eyes were large and blank.

"There!"

She lifted her finger a little.

"What on earth's the matter?"

"It went pop! It just came out of the grass for a moment, then – pop! – it went down again!"

"What went pop?" Gédémus remained still with his sausage in his hand.

"The tree."

"The tree? . . . Aren't you a bit crazy?"

"Yes, the tree! What we've been seeing since the morning. That black thing, first with a branch on one side and then with a branch on the other. The thing about which I said to you three or four times: 'What's that?' and you said: 'It's a tree; come on!' It's there again. It popped out again!"

"It's in your imagination, silly girl. How can a tree go pop like that?"

"It did anyhow. Perhaps it's not a tree."

"What could it be, then, in this place?"

"I really don't know; but it did pop, I'm sure. It was not in my imagination. I saw it clear enough."

"Don't start your silly fusses."

Arsule kept quiet but stopped eating. Her daisy-like eyes were still wide open. Gédémus ate another mouthful then looked at her out of the corner of his eye and, seeing her keep so still, he said:

"Wait a minute, I'll go and see," and he got up.

He walked a few steps into the grass, but then turned round and said:

"You'd better give me my knife."

Then he went off with his open knife in his hand. He walked slowly, looking on either side as if he were afraid of treading on a snake.

Arsule huddled in her nest of grass. She cried out to him:

38

"It's over there!"

She pointed to the exact place.

He went there.

"If it's here, you were dreaming . . . . There's nothing!"

He returned. He appeared worried. From time to time he looked back.

He laid his knife in the box.

"There's nothing . . . . However, if you feel uneasy here, let's go. We'll finish eating on the way, and we'll eat all the better for it this evening at La Trinité."

As soon as they had got up and stepped along the track, they had to reckon with the wind. It was blowing full in their faces and clapped its big, warm hand on their mouths as if to prevent them from breathing. They were used to it. They just turned their faces round a little, to drink in the air on one side, as swimmers do, and thus moved on a good way. It was tiring but not so bad. The wind began to scratch their eyes with its nails. Then it tried to tear off their clothes; it nearly blew off Gédémus's coat. Arsule was pulling on the strap, leaning forward. The wind entered her bodice, as if at home there. It flowed between her breasts and stole down to her belly as might a hand; it flowed between her loins, cooling her like a bath. Her back and hips were all freshened with the wind. She felt its freshness on her but also its warmth, as if it were full of flowers, and its tickling, as if she were being whipped with handfuls of hay. That is what people do during the hay-making season. It puts some women all in a flutter, as the men well know.

Then, suddenly, she began to think about men. It was the wind that had been playing the part of a man for a while.

Gédémus, in two bounds, caught up with Arsule.

"Did you see anything again?"

He seemed to be disturbed.

Arsule looked round at him with a tender and caressing eye.

"No, nothing more."

Her body was fermenting like new wine.

*

39

All of a sudden, the dull truce of twilight fell on them; the wind dropped and there was a hush all round, crisp as a watermelon.

The night walked forth towards them, sweeping before it the scattered houses of La Trinité. They were nearly there.

Formerly La Trinité was a hamlet packed into the midst of the plateau, with a dozen houses huddled together. They stood back to back, showing the earth the great open doors of their barns and the teeth of their harrows. They were sturdy enough. But at that place the plateau really became something quite unusual. As far as the eye could see it was huge and barren, and so flat that it made you feel sick and hanker after anything which went upwards. It was like sleep. It held your head and gripped all round your eyes. After a time you could no longer bear it and threw stones at the sky, just to see them go upwards.

It was almost in the middle of the heap of dilapidated houses that Gédémus had discovered a small barn still standing erect. It was where they used to spend their first night. They had to step over crumbled pieces of wall and push aside branches of fig trees growing wild. Those branches, now stripped and twisted and chilled by the night, felt like snakes when one touched them.

The barn stood in the middle of that nest of fig trees. It looked like a cellar because the house behind it had fallen in and blocked the windows, because the house in front of it had fallen in too and half blocked the doorway, and they had to stoop to get down into it. Once inside, they were comfortable. They pushed the grinding-machine to the far end.

"Ah!" said Gédémus with a sigh. "Here we are, at last! I'm not sorry for that. The fact is that it is a good step from Sault and, besides, walking on the plateau is not like walking on a road, eh, Arsule?"

The whole of Arsule's right arm was as good as dead. She touched her shoulder where the strap had left a mark which could be felt under the bodice. It hurt. There was no longer a wind to caress her and she was tired. It seemed to her that the fingers of the wind were still upon her and that its great hand was laid on her bare flesh.

"Look into the bottom of the box. I think I put some candles there."

Only a small patch of dirty daylight remained spread across the doorway. There still remained an old wooden door-panel which could be shut if sufficient care was taken of the old hinges. That way they were able to shut out a muggy, grey sky, blurred over by the night. They were at last sheltered. The candle-light was there like a russet fruit on the straw.

"Listen," said Gédémus, "we've gone a long way today, and the wind has buffeted us. Let's open a tin of sardines. Never mind! Let's have a treat! And then we'll have a good drink! We've rushed today as if we had fireworks in our breeches. Pass me the gourd, the one with the wine in it."

They had two gourds which held about two litres each. In one there was wine, in the other water. It was an understood thing that they should be mixed.

"Drink it neat too, Arsule, and pass me the tin of sardines."

As he opened the tin he spilt some oil on his fingers. He licked them.

"They are first rate!"

Arsule had prepared two slices of bread. At that moment it happened again. They had stopped talking and were eating. They were looking at the flame of the candle and thinking their own thoughts. For a while they said to themselves: "It's the wind again." Then they remained as they had before with their mouths full, listening.

And there was nothing to listen to.

They began to eat again; Gédémus's eyes went from the candle to the door. Around the door-panel the frame of grey daylight was no longer to be seen. The shoulder of night was weighing down against the door.

"Are you all right?" asked Gédémus.

"Yes," Arsule answered.

A long spell of silence followed. It had done them good to speak a couple of words. Then, because it lasted too long, the silence became still more unpleasant than the rest, and they started talking again.

41

"Do you want me to open another tin of sardines?" asked Gédémus.

"We have only two, you know, and it's our first day."

It was true: it seemed to them that they had been on the plateau for a long, long time. What had happened before had become so small.

"D'you know what I'm thinking about, Arsule? I'm thinking that in life we go on behaving like fools. When we've got good things, we always want to keep them for the next day . . . for the short time we've got on earth! I don't say that because of the sardines. There! It's all right, we'll eat them tomorrow. Tomorrow's not far off. Though, between now and then, anything might . . . I don't mean that for us. You know, just by way of talking . . . . But, believe me, half the time we're asses. Once it's one thing, then another that falls on you, and then, my friend, it's too late. You're done for! If one knew everything!"

There was still nothing to listen to. Nothing but Gédémus. He seemed to comfort himself by talking. Arsule listened to the words, but beyond she listened also to the silence, because there had indeed been something in that silence which was not natural. And they might well talk and talk, it wouldn't prevent what had happened a few minutes ago from happening again. The proof that Gédémus thought so too was that he glanced at the door from time to time.

"If one knew everything! It's not that I mind much, really. It's just by way of talking, but it's just like me at my age to go running about these suspicious parts . . . . It's not that exactly. I've been this way for over thirty years. I know what I'm doing. I'm no longer a child. It's just by way of talking. I've had a hundred opportunities of taking up a plot of ground, with no more need to go off again. We'd be quietly staying down there, at Sault . . . ."

The candle was half burned. One could not talk all night long like that. When asleep, one hears nothing.

"You're tired, Arsule. Shall we go to sleep?"

First he went as far as the door and listened. Then he half opened it and put his head out to have a look. There was nothing on the plateau. It was all white as far as the eye could see. There was

42

nothing in the sky. The moon, entirely naked, was hovering alone in the middle of the night, like an almond.

They must have slept for a fairly long while. To begin with, they were tired, and, besides, they did not want to hear or see anything more. As Arsule began to fall asleep she no longer knew what she was doing, and her labouring body did things for her. She gently drew near Gédémus and nestled by him, pressing herself against the man's thigh. She pressed the man's thigh between her own thighs and the buds of her breasts rested against Gédémus's back. She went to sleep like that. They must have remained a long time in that position. Suddenly they both wakened.

Things had happened in the meantime. The plateau, the wind, the night, all had had plenty of time to prepare and everything was in tune. Under the door there was a thick silver bar, four fingers wide; it was the moonlight. A night wind with full breath had arisen. It was tearing along at full speed across the whole extent of the plateau, with long moans as if it wanted to swallow up the whole sky. The heath was cracking under its feet, the crushed juniper shrubs were crying out. The fig trees were scratching the walls and their huge stumps were rumbling in the earth under the stones. There were all these noises, but that was not what had wakened them. It was the sound of a footfall accompanied by the flapping of cloth.

"D'you hear?"

"Yes," whispered Arsule.

"Don't move!"

It was close to them. It fumbled along the walls. A stone fell.

"Don't move," Gédémus whispered again to Arsule, who was not moving.

It went through the jumble of fig trees. It stopped to disentangle the cloth. Then footsteps. They huddled against each other without moving. They felt that they must avoid making the straw rustle. Through their gaping mouths they took deep gulps of breath, slowly and noiselessly. They had to remain there in the dark, silent, motionless, like the dark itself. They had to do so. It was no longer a laughing matter. Suddenly they felt that they had to hold their breath.

A shadow had blotted out the silver bar which gleamed under the door. That was clear! It was quite certain this time. It was there in front of them. A slight noise rustled against the door, fingering the wood. It seemed as if a hand was resting against the door-panel to see if it was shut. It was shut. The big stone which held it closed moved slightly. It creaked. Slight as it was, it was all the same a force which had come there to see, which had fumbled.

And then it went. The water of the moon began to flow again, gleaming under the door.

They waited for a long while without speaking, without moving, still part of the darkness itself. Their eyes were wide open and they were looking at the bar of moonlight because there lay the indication.

There was nothing more. Only the wind.

Gédémus still waited for some time before turning round to Arsule. His head and his mouth were quite close to Arsule's head and mouth, and he said to her:

"Did you see?"

"Yes."

"Listen. This afternoon, on the plateau, when I went to have a look at the place where it 'popped,' the grass had been flattened out as if under a weight, under the weight of some animal . . . . It was just rising again . . . . But when I reached the spot it was still flattened down. There you are! And you saw it! There's something against us this time."

The door was open and it was broad daylight.

"Arsule, how could such a country do us any harm? Look at it now. Isn't it beautiful?"

All was iris-blue, earth and sky together, with a cluster of clouds in the west. The young sun made his way, knee-deep in the grass. The wind scattered the dew like a lively colt. It sent up flights of birds which swam for a while among the waves of the sky, as if drunk and dizzy from screaming, and then suddenly dropped, like handfuls of stones.

"Ah! We're fine soldiers, both of us!"

They had brought out the grinding-machine. There it stood on its wheels, in the straight line of a small lane. It was ready to start; Arsule had taken the strap. The day was radiant, like a brand-new silver coin.

"We've only to walk towards the sun, and in two hours we'll reach Pimprenelle. From there up to the end of the heath it'll take three hours more, but the morning's still young. All things considered, with the rest we'll have for lunch and a bit of a nap to make up the time we lost last night, we should get there long before evening. All things considered."

But he had not considered everything, and they set out.

It must have been about the middle of the morning when Gédémus turned his head to look behind him. La Trinité lay at the bottom of the moor, like a small heap of cold cinders. Later on he looked round again. La Trinité could no longer be seen and only the sky was in its place. In front of him there was the sky too, and the sky again on either side. Under his feet there was that porous ground which echoed like the ceiling of a cellar; no more grass, but only twisted juniper shrubs. Now they stood on the open plateau just as on the open sea.

Arsule stopped.

"It's just popped up again – there, in front."

Gédémus scratched his head.

"Far?"

"No! Just in front."

In front of them was only flat grass.

"Well, then," he said, "let's turn a bit to the right." So they left the regular road for lost regions where the sky had been so tightly stuck against the earth that they had to fight their way with their heads to pass between the two.

The next morning found them wan as naked birds. They were lying in a nest of grass, huddled against each other. When daylight touched them they lifted their heads and their sleepless eyes recognized the earth. Above the plateau a slight mist rose like smoke.

"I know where we are," said Gédémus. "We're near Aubignane. Not so bad, Arsule. Beyond there's Vachères. Not so bad."

The sun gave them life again and they felt the strength to get up. Arsule passed her arm into the strap and they started off again. Gédémus knew that straight ahead the plateau suddenly broke and that there was Aubignane – a few cottages, a valley with trees and water. Not so bad.

The dawn was warm. To the east the sky was open like an oven door. No more grass; the plateau sloped down a little and the wind had heaped up all its sand on that slope.

Arsule tugged like a donkey with all the strength of her haunches and loins.

That excitement of her flesh, that labour of her blood, had just returned to her, as if it were a curse. Her breasts were again like tree-buds. She pulled at her bodice because it rubbed against her nipples and worried her. She sniffed, the better to catch the smell of Gédémus, who was sweating. She was also sweating and she bent down towards her arm-pits to catch her own smell. She moaned to herself: "Mamma, Mamma," as if she were afraid.

Aubignane was the same colour as the plateau. One could not see it beforehand, then, all of a sudden, one arrived.

"I passed this way once, long ago. There were still a few people here then. There was Jean Blanc, who lived in the church square. Let's go and see."

There was nothing but grass on the church square. Jean Blanc's door was nailed up.

"There was Paul Soubeyran in the next street. There was also Ozias Bonnet, who ran the grocery."

They found a doorless house which was dark inside and sounded like a grotto as soon as they set foot on the threshold: it was a shell and nothing more. When their eyes had grown accustomed to the dark, they saw at the far end a sort of tree of gold and light. It was a great crevice which had cleft the main wall from foundations to tiles.

"There was also a man they called Panturle, living with his

mother, but outside the village, down below there, near the cypress. Come. We'll go down."

There also the door was closed. Yet there was a block on which wood had been chopped. They saw fresh cuts on the block, and a live path going straight under the door. There was also a blue woollen belt hanging from a branch of the cypress, swaying in the wind. But when they examined it they found it was an old one.

"Oho there!" Gédémus cried out.

Then he said:

"That man's not been gone a long time."

Soft green grass grew in front of the house. There stood the cypress too, and, as if on purpose, it was singing with its tree-voice, its sweet-sounding voice, inviting to the ear. Then there were bees which had lived under a tile and were humming in the air. And then, like a miracle, so unexpected that it made them rub their eyes, there was a small lilac tree in full blossom.

"Let's rest, Arsule, let's rest."

Gédémus, lying on the ground, stretched himself out like a dog. "One could almost sleep."

No, she would not be able to sleep with that longing within her, like water carrying everything away. Her heart was like a crumbling clod of earth. She sat in the grass, with daisies between her legs. She was only an empty bag of skin; she listened to that bitter water, like fire, singing deep down within her.

She opened her bodice and took out her breasts. They were hard and hot and she had one in either hand . . . .

Just at that moment she saw a pool of blood, thick as a peony, on the white threshold of the door.

IV

PANTURLE PICKED UP FROM THE STRAW AN APPLE FROM the previous autumn. It was cold and green. He warmed it in his hand and then with his mouth, blowing on it before biting into it.

He was sitting in front of his door. Things had changed since Mamèche left. In one of the corners a lilac twig was ready to bloom, and the wind from the plain had brought a big bee which was full of excitement and had started sniffing the tiles. But it would die. It was a few days too early.

He had gone to lie in wait for a fox. It had to be done with a good deal of silence and few gestures. One had to hide in the hill and listen. If one knew how to read the noises of the air, one learned that it slept there, that it went from a certain place to another, that it hunted quails or was on the track of partridges. After that, it was child's play to set the trap.

While looking out for the fox, Panturle met the wind, a good wind right in his face, full and free; no longer the low wind which enjoyed itself tossing things about, but a good, broad-shouldered wind which hustled the whole countryside. Seeing it like that, Panturle said to himself: "That's something like a wind!"

He did not quite know how it happened. He had been lying in the grass, looking out for a fox. Then he had gradually let his thoughts slip towards something else. It must be said that the place where he was lying was that solitary hillock, facing the south, over which passed all the movement of the air. The wind pressed all its weight upon him, thumping big, heavy blows, then flew away, purring like a cat. He was lying flat on his belly and the wind squeezed him like a sponge. His thoughts about the yelping fox for which he lay in wait seemed to flow from him into the grass, and the earth sucked them up. The other thoughts which lurked within his body like vinegar or soft water also flowed from him, pressed as he was by the wind. And again the earth and the grass sucked them up.

There he lay, suddenly empty.

The wind rapped with its finger against him as against a barrel, to see whether there was any juice left. No, Panturle sounded like an empty barrel under the finger of the wind.

When he came home it was almost night. There might never have been any foxes on earth.

He realized that it was almost night, for as he walked with his head upright against the wind, he saw the sun poking its horns through the small window of the steeple. He felt as if he had been washed from top to bottom, like a sheet scrubbed by a brush. He felt all white and full of new life. He walked the earth with a clean heart.

All the same, the next day he heard the fox calling. It was due to an age-long habit which made his head work mechanically by its own impetus. It came from Valgast, then from Chaume-Bâtard, which meant that the animal had passed somewhere among the rocks in the hollow of the uplands. That was all right. The trap was of good steel; its jaw could snap perfectly. He took some offal of putrid rabbit, oiled the spring of the trap, and everything was ready.

Panturle got up. He noticed the hawthorn at the brook. It was new also. It was in full bloom, as if covered with foam. As he stood there a ball of feathers and cries struck his breast, fell to the ground, divided and sprang up again from the grass in the shape of two sparrows.

"Giddy birds! Where are your eyes?"

At the same moment the wind passed its warm arm round his waist and took him along. The reason he gave himself was that it was too early to go and set his trap. The truth was that he felt as if he were going out for a walk with a friend.

There was Caroline bleating. It was no longer her old she-goat's voice but the soft little quavering of a baby goat. She complained in this way to all the four corners of the air. She moaned in front of the cypress and then in front of the hawthorn bush. She browsed on the first lilac blossoms. This morning only two or three drops of yellow milk could be pressed out of her teats and remained in her coat. Panturle tried again with his thumb. Caroline reared, broke loose, and moaned up against the small window which was blowing out its breath like a flower of the wind.

The bowl was empty.

"Well, then, Caroline," Panturle asked, "well, is that all?"

She came back to him, trembling all over, pushed her rocky head against what she felt to be the animal in him, caressing gently and whining.

"Well, Caroline, well?" Panturle repeated.

The hawthorn bush, on which the sun rested as soon as it had risen above the hill, had a nightingale in its foliage. It seemed as if the shrub itself were warbling.

In the small meadow the grass waved gently, though there was no wind. It was through this that Panturle noticed a snake with new skin wriggling along. When it reached the end of the meadow, it looked round; one could see that it had nothing else to do but to glide with its whole body across the fresh verdure. A small swarm of bees had now collected beneath the eaves of the tiled roof, seeking shelter. They looked like a handful of chaff blown about by the wind.

Near noon a big, strange dog appeared and hung about on the border of the meadow. It was lean and all bones, like the stump of a vine. Its red mouth sought the drift of the wind. It went to the brook and drank. After drinking it raised its head and looked at Panturle for a while. Then it began to drink again. The water could be heard going down its throat in great gulps. It accumulated with the wind inside the dog's skin. Suddenly a scent must have passed by, for the dog darted after it.

One felt that the earth had been passionately working on something which was now bursting forth in the moaning of the grass under the tramping of heavy animals. Females, no doubt, heavy with pregnancy. There were still a number of light and lean males bounding about, but there were mostly heavy animals, as if swollen, passing slowly through the glades, searching about the bushes, and rustling the dry leaves under the oaks.

They made Panturle stop when he came across them, and watch them without moving. They would hustle off clumsily towards some covert and would huddle together there, panting for breath, with their eyes trembling like flowers in the wind.

"They are females."

He would leave them in peace, for he was a hunter and knew that they carried his quarry in their bellies.

"What a passion the earth has!" he exclaimed.

He felt uneasy and bitter. He suddenly realized he was alone. Caroline no longer had any milk.

"She needs a billygoat," he said.

That night he had a dream which made him toss and turn and which worried him as if he were being tickled in the fold of his elbow.

Before going to sleep, he thought of his solitude and then of the time he had spent with Gaubert and Mamèche. Then he thought ardently of Mamèche herself. If only she had been younger . . . . Mad to think of that, but then there was that great hatred which the world had against him, right from the sun to the grass! That mad strength which spring had put into the hollow of his loins and which boiled there like water over the fire! . . . If Mamèche had still been there, he would have waited for the day. He would have waited for the day, because that night was too evil for his understanding and he was no longer sure of his gestures. Once the day had come, he would have gone to her and said:

"Since you want to, go and find me a woman. Go, since you know where to find those who would be willing."

But after all, he thought, that was perhaps the reason she had gone. She was stubborn in her ideas.

There was a knock at the door.

With a bound he went to open it. The solitary night greeted him.

He went back to bed. He fell asleep and soon he had the woman whom he wanted lying against him. Her skin was white and she pressed against him from his knees to his breast. He came awake as a block of wood rises to the surface after a plunge into water. He was lying on his belly. He turned over again on his back.

Then it came back to him again, more slowly, as if from further away, but it came back: a house to which he used to go at the time of his military service, behind the town slaughter-house. Every time he went he had a fight with the artillerymen. He had to go over a small bridge. In the dirty stream underneath, the water slept among the detritus and offal. The water was black with a silky skin of all colours. There was everything in it: old guts, stiffened pieces of skinned oxfoot with hoofs swollen as big as heads.

He bounded on his mattress like a fish. He awoke and went to the window. Outside there was a beautiful moon. Feeling quite ill, he stayed there against that beautiful moon which made the basin of light formed by the window-frame overflow almost to the hearth.

An animal came to play in the meadow. It must have been a she-badger. She lay down on her back, with her belly upturned. It was a fine, big belly, as velvety as the night and both full and heavy.

That morning he again tried to milk Caroline. The udder seemed in his hand like a small dead animal. Not even the first yellow drop of milk came out . . . it was dried up.

He punched her in the ribs. Caroline was taken by surprise but avoided a second blow by hollowing her loins. Why had the man struck?

He still wanted to strike. Had it not been Caroline – the goat – he would have struck again . . . . If only it had been a man, he would have struck again. It did him good. For otherwise he felt bitter and all in bloom, like the hawthorn bush . . . .

Later on, he caught the fox: it was a young one. It had been caught in the trap only a few moments before. It must have been nibbling at the bait warily because it knew the contraption, and then, hearing Panturle's step, its bite had been a little quicker, less calculated, and the jaw of the trap had snapped on its neck. It was dead. A long steel thorn had passed through its neck. Under its coat it was still warm and heavy with food. Panturle took it out of the trap, covering his fingers with blood. The sight of the blood quite upset him. He held the fox by its hind legs with one paw in each hand. All of a sudden he tightened his grip on the paws and with a sharp gesture opened out his arms, and the fox was ripped open with its bones cracking all along its spine down to the middle of its breast. A good quantity of swollen guts rolled out and brought with it a warm smell, like that of dung. It made Panturle's eyes swim in his head madly.

Perhaps he closed them.

He blindly thrust his big hand into the animal's belly and fumbled about in the blood for those soft things which burst between his fingers. They squirted like crushed grapes. It was so good that he uttered a subdued cry.

He went back home. The dead animal warmed his fist like a mouth.

He hung up the fox in front of his doorstep to flay it. His hands were covered to the wrist with blood. There was even a streak that trickled, dried, and trickled again along his arm, across the hair. There was also blood on the doorstep. He bore down with his pointed knife on the skin. The knife seemed to hesitate for a moment,

then suddenly to make up its mind and plunge. He had to hold it back.

It was good to feel a knife cutting in!

It might have been a vixen.

With little ones, like white walnuts. A string of little ones!

It might have been that mother badger with her heavy belly floating in the fountain of the moon.

"What am I thinking about? I must be a bit crazy!"

The wind entered his shirt and came against his skin, coiling about and squirming like a serpent. The heap of guts lay in the grass, just under the fragrance of the lilac tree.

He fumbled about inside the fox as in a pocket. That heavy and juicy thing which was like a ripe fruit, and which he was now crushing, smelt bitter, like hawthorn blossom. It was the liver. A stream of green gall spurted out on his thumb . . . .

Suddenly he was brought back to earth. A strong hand clasped him by the neck and made him realize that he was standing at Aubignane, in front of his house, flaying a fox like a blackguard.

Steps could be heard in the village lane. He listened. Yes, it was a footstep on the stones.

Mamèche?

No, it was the voice of a man, then another answering voice which made his very heart throb, and made his face hot with shame at having wallowed with his hands in blood.

He unhooked the animal and went into the house. He shut the door gently and pushed home the bolt.

He no longer heard any noise. He knew that they had lain down in the grass. He bent down. He unlaced his big shoes. He walked barefoot to the door. Yes, they were there.

How could he see them? . . . From the loft . . . .

He climbed the steps quietly, balancing himself with both his arms outstretched. The attic window was at the floor level. He lay down. He crawled over towards it.

He saw them. He saw her.

He remained in the shade. They were in the sun. It was like

hunting. She was young.

He rose with one bound, not caring about the noise he made, and rushed towards the stairs, for down there the woman had opened her bodice and was holding her breasts in her hands.

He stumbled against the kneading-trough and rolled over.

"God damn!" he cried and punched the wooden trough as if it were a human chest.

He got up and bumped his head against the sloping roof. It seemed as if his mouth were full of that hawthorn blossom. He spat. The shadow of the staircase was starred all over with the dancing golden stars that came out of his eyes. It was a mass of red in which he stumbled. His knees gave way under him as he jumped, and he slid down, partly on his back and partly on his elbows, as he was carried away by the powerful impulse of his whole body.

With two more leaps he upset his cauldron . . . .

Oh, how long his hand took to find the bolt! One of his fingernails broke on the iron. He tore open the creaking door . . . . Nobody!

Just the cypress, the lilac bush with its blossom half eaten by Caroline, the bees in the roof, buzzing up and down, and a gentle breeze in the belfry up there.

He sniffed heavily, just like a wild boar taken by surprise, swallowing the air that whistled in his wide-open nostrils.

His chest was puffed out and he brought down his fist on it with a strong blow.

But there on the ground a circle of grass was pressed down, like a nest. The woman had been there. It was certainly not just the wind, as last night.

In the lane a branch was moving from left to right; if it had been swayed by the wind it would have moved up and down.

A noise of rolling stones.

The branch and the noise of the stones showed him the direction.

It was that way . . . .

Right.

In that direction there was only one way they could be going: first to Plantades, then from Plantades to Moulières, down past Soubeyran below the waterfall of the Gaudissart brook.

Right.

He opened his mouth to fill himself with good, soft air. Should he run after them? No, he knew!

There was too much daylight and that daylight protected the man and the woman. What could he do in daylight but speak with man's words? He did not know how to speak with man's words for that sort of thing. He was too full of seething strength and needed the gestures of animals.

He went home and put on his shoes again. He took his fox-flaying knife and came back under the cypress. Then he swallowed another two or three gulps of air and went off on his path of spring.

That was it!

There was the path, the track of the woman. It was there, along that thin thread of earth, trembling between the shoots of grass. He was shaken by deep, noiseless laughter, his hunter's laugh. He laughed at being able to read that thing written in the air and on the ground. It was the path, too, that made him laugh, the path that had been wound in the hills like the thong of a whip, of which he held the handle. With a good whip and a sharp stroke of the wrist one could pluck a flower two metres away, in the meadow, up there! It was the same thing here. But bigger.

It made him laugh until he slobbered. He wiped his mouth with the back of his hand which was cemented with blood. He also had fox blood on his mouth.

Spring clung to his shoulders like a big cat.

The Gaudissart brook flowed along for some time over flattened grass, then began to beat against rocks, and finally dived into the hill. It cut through great stone banks, buried itself in the hill, and there purred away in grey twilight. That was its nest. Sometimes it swelled its fine belly covered with scaly foam. Sometimes it stretched itself out between two sharp bones of rock. Sometimes, when the night was dark, all that could be seen was its big, grass-coloured eye on the watch.

Panturle knew all that through and through. Even when it was pitch-dark he could put his foot on the right stone, stretch out his hand and clasp the right root. Then he would press his back against the oily flank of the rocks and pass by.

It was a short cut.

At the other end of the gorge, the sky, like an iron wedge, cut into the hill. He began to see better there. The Gaudissart glided swiftly along as if in a well-polished runnel of schist. In there it was drawn out at full length, streaked by long rays of light which shot out of the darkness like arrows and curled up into the daylight at the other end. It was drawn out to such an extent that someone seemed to be standing up above on the plateau, pulling it by the tail, while someone else down below in the plain was pulling at its head, as if it were a snake being flayed. As it came nearer and nearer to the daylight, it seemed to change into silk and become soft and glossy, puffing itself with air and wind. Finally it lay folded on the hillside, like a neckerchief put out to dry on a bank.

For the Gaudissart, earth-eater as it was, had not eaten away enough of the plateau. Thus it arrived at the other end at a height of forty metres, and then leapt down. It leapt three times, over three rounded steps between cushions of moss. First it took the small jump of a child, then in one bound it darted over the rock and flung itself down into six metres of space. It came to rest on its resilient haunches, rolled for twenty metres down a slope, and then, with a graceful spring, curved like a bow, it went down into the plain of Soubeyran, in the midst of a rumbling pool.

Down below, the path went round the pool, forded the brook with three stepping-stones, then went off and crushed its way along wild meadows.

Panturle stopped at the issue of the brook just above the waterfall, and lay in wait under a pine tree. From there he could see the outskirts of the wood and, according to his plan, as soon as they stepped out of covert, he would be able to follow them with his eyes. Time went by and made his desire swell within him and fill him up. It had crushed all the man within him. There remained in the grass only the overwhelming male. His eyes did not leave the edge of the wood. Nothing had come out but a couple of magpies learning to fly, with the feathers of their rumps open like fans, and then dropping into the dry hay like balls.

He pursed his lips instead of laughing, sniffed, spat, and then crept forward in the grass on all fours to the edge of the fall. The pine tree hung over the water. It was ill-treated by both the wind and the water. The bark on the lower part of its trunk was all mouldy. Panturle hugged the sticky trunk and scrambled up with a scissor-like motion of his knees. He threw forward his big hands with fingers full of resin which clasped round the branches, pulled himself up by his arms, and slid up with his loins. Only the wind and his desire seemed to resound through his blank head.

He settled at last, squatting like an animal on the long branch overhanging the void. He could see well from there. The branch cracked. He could see well; but the effort of watching made him tremble all over. His long muscles quivered, uncontrolled, inside his flesh, just like long ropes with buckets tied to them at the bottom of wells.

Nothing.

The branch cracked. There he was with all his weight among the leaves.

Suddenly the branch gave a long groan and bent. With the instinct of an animal he jerked his back and threw up his hands towards a branch above him. But it was just as if it flew away, and he fell.

He was struck hard in the back by the cold hand of the brook and he saw its long white fingers close on him. In a moment the water glided round him and enveloped him with its thick, slippery body. He struck at it with his arms and legs, but it seized him by the waist, crushed his nose, and threw him over, pressing his shoulders down on the flat stones in its depths.

He arched his back and, shooting out his arms, springing like a fish, he darted upwards. His mouth bumped against a mass of air, which seemed as hard as a stone. He swallowed a great gulp, filling his lungs, then, in his turn, he pressed with all his weight on the shoulder of the water. He threw his hand out towards the bank and dug his fingers into the earth. It was loose and yielded under his grasp, and scattered with bits of rushes round the fight.

Again, the powerful grip of the water held him round the waist. The brook suddenly seized him, carried him away, and threw him headlong over the ledge.

He fell on the first ledge full on his belly like a toad and immediately began to struggle again. But in reality he moved his arms and legs very slowly – so slowly that they might have been stuck in glue. The relentless water moved its own arms and legs with redoubled strength and foamed with anger.

Then he was thrown over the second ledge like a bundle.

He rolled down the last slope without offering more resistance. He rolled among water and moss, with the image of the soldiers' house and the smell of carrion like flowers rotting at the door. The flowers, full of blood and pus and swarming with flies, became magnified in his mind.

Golden flies swarmed in his eyes.

It seemed as if the water closed his mouth with a handful of cold tripe.

Finally he was hurled right down into the pool.

He had begun to live again a few moments ago, but he still kept his eyes closed.

A persistent quiet sound and a freshness stole over him; voices of several trees were talking together. He said to himself: "It's the wind." It was then that he came back to life.

He recognized the night by the taste of the air in his nostrils. Then he opened his eyes, but he had not thought of the moon, and the large moon pierced his sensitive eyes like a knife. He quickly shut his eyes again, but he had had time to see in a twinkling that his head was lying in the grass. What was he doing there? He remained motionless for a good while, wondering what had happened, then he recognized the taste in his mouth. It had a smell of mud and water-moss. He moved his tongue slowly and worked his jaws, as if to chew the smell and see if it did not remind him of something. Small grains of sand grated between his teeth.

Shortly afterwards he noticed that he was lying on his belly on cold stones. This astonished him, for as a rule he never lay like that because it gave him colic.

It was certainly small gravel that he had in his mouth. Besides, he heard far away in the wind the rumble of the waterfall, and it all became clear to him, especially as little by little he recovered his senses. He remembered the crash and the pine branch and he saw himself again hanging from it like a monkey. His shoulder hurt him and he heaved a deep sigh, half opening an eye to see if he was really lying in the grass on dry earth.

It was really the earth, and it made him feel better. Across the clear moon he saw the shadow of a poplar.

He thought:

"If I stay like this on my belly, I'll catch my death of colic." He tried to turn and fell over in a heap. The moon set her white finger on his eyelids. A voice near him said:

"He's moved."

He opened his eyes without troubling any more about the moon, and lifted his head; it sounded like the woman's voice.

And it was she.

She was sitting there in the grass beside him. She was looking at him. She had spoken; nobody had answered.

"Well, are you better?" she asked.

He did not understand immediately, and then replied:

"Better? Yes; and you?"

"Oh, I had a great fright. I could not go to sleep. So I came just to see how you were getting on. You were just turning over. So I thought: 'He's getting better.' It took a weight off my chest."

She was in the moonlight. He could see her well: her face was pointed and pale like a big turnip, almost no chin, a long smooth nose like a stone, eyes like plums, round, velvety, and sparkling, her lip swollen by those two front teeth which stuck out boldly when she laughed. She was lovely!

"You're very kind," said Panturle. "So it's you who pulled me out onto the grass."

He spat to free his mouth of that taste of gravel and water.

She approached on her knees in the grass, right up to Panturle.

"I'll come nearer so as not to wake him up. Yes, it's me, too, who pulled you out. It happened just as we were coming out of the wood. We had the waterfall right in front of our eyes and we were looking at it. Then we saw a big branch fall, and then something like a bundle of linen. He said: 'They've let the washing drop.' I said: 'Washing? Why, it's a man.' He said: 'A man? Not likely!' I saw what had happened right away. I said to him again: 'It's a man!'

"That was just when you were being swept down the great fall, and we saw you quite well, stretched out to your full length on the falling water. Then we ran to your help. You were darting along, all stiff, under the water, like a big fish, and the current swept you to the bank. He and I pulled you out onto the grass. You vomited water right away, and he said to me: 'He's not dead. He'll come round.' We waited for a while. You didn't come round. Then he said: 'As it's now dark it's all the same to us if we sleep here or elsewhere. Only we must move away a bit from the waterfall, for here it's as wet as if it were raining.' And so we came as far as here. We dragged you along in the grass, because you're heavy, and he's an old man, and I, as you see, I'm only a woman. Look! You can still see the traces in the grass."

It was true. In the meadow there was still a wide track of flattened grass. Panturle lay at the end of it like a wagon at the end of its track.

"Did it give you much trouble?" he asked.

"Yes, of course; you're heavy."

She went on:

"You are heavy, but we pulled you along by the arms; your legs trailed behind. Then we lighted a fire. Do you smell it?"

He could smell burnt thyme and oak stump.

"We tried to dry you. Then you began to breathe again and he said: 'Leave him now; we'll go to sleep.' He fell asleep at once, but I was unable to and I came to see how you were getting on. Then you moved. That's all."

*

After a while he felt uneasy, lying at full length in front of that woman. He tried to get up. His shoulder hurt him, then his hip. But he soon realized it was nothing serious and he managed to sit up.

"Ah! That's better," he said.

The woman was somewhat smaller than he. He lowered his head to look at her and in reply she raised her pointed face.

When she did that the moon shone fully on her.

She asked:

"Well, then, whoever you are, are you from these parts, or from a long way off, like us?"

"I come from here," Panturle said.

"This place, where we are now?"

"Not quite. A bit to the left. From that place, there," he said after a time, when he had recognized the black mass of the hill. "There," and he pointed it out to her. "From Aubignane."

"From Aubignane? I couldn't have guessed it. There's no longer anybody there."

"There is. There's me, and you were in front of my house."

"Ah! The house with the blood?"

She recoiled towards the grass and the shadow of the grass. Her hands clutched at her knees. She murmured:

"There was blood on the doorstep. We thought some evil had occurred and we ran away . . . ."

A great gust of wind, full of the smell of hawthorn, passed over the silence.

"I was flaying a fox," Panturle said.

"Ah! That was why."

"Yes."

"When one lives alone," he said after a while, "one is wicked, or one turns so. I was not like that before. I must have got like it since I've been alone, and it's partly because of the weather also. This hot weather has a curious effect on me. I'm not like that usually."

She looked at him.

"No, you don't seem to be like that."

Panturle was shaken by a long shiver.

"You're cold?"

"No. But all this wet stuff's taking my warmth away . . . ."

He still had something to say. He hesitated for a while, then it seemed to him quite simple and all right, so he added:

"I'll strip. It'll be better."

And she said:

"Yes, you'd better." Then: "You mustn't catch cold." He peeled off his coat and shirt as if they were skin, and he sat there, naked under his hair.

He lay back in the grass and said:

"It's warm; touch it . . . "

She touched the grass, just where he was lying.

"Yes," she said.

She also touched his flesh, which was still rather cold. "Won't you be cold?"

"Oh, I'm used to it! It's pretty warm here; besides, the grass is good and the air's good, and anyhow I soon warm up. There, you can feel it already."

He took her hand and put it on his breast at the spot where he had the trembling animal within him.

She felt the big swelling movement of his ribs, as if he were a basket being opened. She touched the thick tuft of hair and under it she really felt his warmth.

"It's true," she said, withdrawing her hand gently.

They remained silent awhile; she even forced herself to speak a little.

"We knocked at your door. And you, where were you?"

"I was inside."

"So you did not answer? That wasn't kind. Why did you do that?"

"Oh, because . . . "

"So that's what you're like? And suppose we had needed help?"

"That's true; but I was ashamed."

"Why?"

"Well, it's hard to know why. I was ashamed, that's all."

She watched him naked on the grass, with the moonlight bathing one side of him.

"But why? After all, it was we who pulled you out of the pool.

What would you have done without us? ... So you remained indoors, locked in, behind the walls, without stirring, listening to us without saying a word. We might have needed something. Are you ashamed of us?"

That made Panturle sit up and begin to speak. He took the woman's hand in his hand. He spoke loud. The woman said to him: "Speak lower!" and nodded with her head towards a dark corner under the willows where somebody appeared to be lying. She did not withdraw her hand. On the contrary, after a while, he no longer had to hold it; she had closed her fingers on Panturle's hand as if on the nose of a friendly dog. And he went on in low tones:

"I'm more willing than most folk to do a good turn."

She had closed her fingers on Panturle's hand. She felt the skin which was like bark with its warts and scars. Sometimes his big forefinger, in sympathy with what he was saying, worked its way over her small fingers, set them apart, slipped between them and squeezed them. Sometimes it was his thumb which pressed on the sensitive hollow of her palm as if it wanted to burst it and enter into and pass through it. Sometimes all his big fingers together squeezed the whole of her little hand.

It shed warmth into her whole body as if, of a sudden, summer with all its crops were lying on her.

He sat there under the moon as if beneath the spout of a fountain. He had big muscles which made shadows along his arms and hips and the skin of his thighs. The hair on his skin was like the coat of a black goat.

She listened; she heard the dull thumping of her blood which seemed to be tramping on her with a heavy heel.

She passed her left hand across the night to feel the man's firm wrist, which was against her right hand. It was all knotted like a gnarled branch. It filled her left hand with warm flesh which was supple and finely nerved.

"I can't explain . . . . They all have their women. Such a passion has seized the earth . . . such a passion!"

She drew a little nearer the man. She drew nearer surreptitiously, leaning towards him, for she did not dare to approach openly. That man's wrist which attached her to him, and which she held in both her hands, was solid flesh, living and warm. It was a bridge over which the man's desire passed into her.

He felt her drawing near; the knot of his hands tightened, the big cord of his wrist vibrated and drew her further towards him. She slipped through the grass and was with him.

All the channels of her blood began to sing like the network of the streams and rivers of the earth. She laid her head on the hair of his breast. She heard the heart and the faint cracking of that basket of ribs which carried the heart like a beautiful fruit on leaves.

Then that weight of water which she had on her shoulders and which was the man's arm became heavy. Like a bundle of hay, she fell back into that arm and lay down in the grass.

First there was a sharp gust and a wailing of the wind from the depths of the wood, the moaning of the sky, then an owl hooting as it alighted on the grass. A wild turtle-dove began to coo.

"There's the dawn."

They said that, one after the other, without looking at each other. Their bodies were now filled with calm and their hearts, like poppies, were at rest.

Yonder, under the poplars, the grinding-machine was attached in a quiet, grassy meadow.

He picked up his corduroys. The velvet was still sodden. He wrung his shirt, tied it round his waist, then put on his shoes. She watched him. She knew what was going to happen; it was so perfectly simple.

"Come!" said Panturle. "We're going home."

And she walked behind him along the path.

PART TWO

I

"THIS CONFOUNDED EARTH!" SAID PANTURLE AS HE came in. "It won't budge. It's harder than stone. It's been abandoned too long. It's all bunged up. One can't even get the blade in."

He looked at his plough. It was the small plough of a poor man, one of those implements that the ploughman draws by throwing himself backwards.

"What's the use of this? All it does is to scratch the top a bit."

Arsule was very much troubled by this news. She looked at Panturle, at the plough, and at the hump of the hill swelling up outside the window.

"Well, then?" she asked.

"Well, then, when all's said and done," Panturle answered, "as I've got to go over there anyhow for the seeds and to see about Caroline, I'll go today. I'll look up Jasmin to get in touch with old Gaubert. He's got the secret of the plough. I'll ask him to make me one. He'll do it willingly for me. It's his passion. I'll ask L'Amoureux if

69

he'll lend me his horse. It's still early. They won't have started yet, and it'll do. You'll see."

"If you're going off," said Arsule, "then you'd do well to put on a clean shirt."

The big kneading-trough had been put in its place under the window. The table was in the corner, shining all over and washed down like a big, square rock after the rain. The hearth was swept. There were three odd plates on the board of the sink. On the mantelpiece was a box of matches. It was from this box that everything started.

Before that, he struck a light with flint and tow or tree pith. It either took or did not. It required patience and was accompanied by many a "Damn my luck!"

One day Arsule said: "If only we had some matches . . . ."

Panturle went off early over the hills. When dawn came he was already on the road, away over there on the other side, almost in sight of the Vachères belfry. He waited there for the mail-coach. He stopped it and asked Michel to get out.

"Come here a minute and let's have a word," he said to him. "Do you think you could sell this hare-skin for me?"

"Perhaps I might."

Sauteiron, the fat horse-dealer, was in the coach. He cried out: "Bring your skin here, man!"

He handed him six francs. Panturle said: "That's all right."

And Michel added: "That's not dear. When you've got some more, keep one for me at that price. I want to make myself a cap."

Panturle handed Michel the six francs, saying: "There. Get me some matches; big boxes."

"For all that?"

"Yes. I'll wait for you here this evening."

That is how Arsule got her matches. She was very pleased with them. She placed them in the dry cupboard. After that she made him put the kneading-trough in its place, for it was heavy. Then she searched the cupboard and brought out trousers and jackets that had belonged to Panturle's father and had been left there folded up since his death. She saw which were in good condition. She also found some needles and an old card of thread, and she said to Panturle: "You might sharpen the scissors for me." When she got up and went out of the room, one would have thought that mulberry leaves had been left to dry there. The bits were all scattered on the floor. But she had no time to clear them up. She was in a hurry. She went and sat in the grass with a big bundle of stuff under her arm. When Panturle came back he found a pair of trousers all patched up and ready to wear and a jacket almost finished. He looked at the jacket. It had the buttons of a hunter's coat, big, brass buttons with figures of animals.

"You're a cunning one!" he said to her.

She also found some old bodices, some wide skirts with ample folds, and some shawls, which she arranged for herself. Then she found, in a kneading-trough of the disused back room, three sheets which were whiter than water. They were lying like fine wheat at the bottom of the trough. Fortunately it was made of good oak, two fingers thick, without a crack, otherwise the rats would have been at them. That decided her. She had been wanting sheets for some time. She went down and looked for Panturle. He was cutting wood.

"D'you know what we ought to do?" she asked.

"No," he replied.

"Well, it's like this," she said. "That straw mattress we're sleeping on downstairs, it's hardly good enough for animals, and it rather upsets me sleeping there where everyone can see."

"Where nobody can see," he replied. "There's nothing and nobody here."

"I know," she said, "but it makes no difference. I really don't like it. We ought to use the room with the cupboard. We'd feel more at ease. There's a wooden bed there, all in pieces. We could easily put it together and take the straw mattress upstairs. We'd be more comfortable."

They did that. When she undid the bed in the evening it was as white as the heart of a lily. She had put on the sheets.

"Well, I never!" said Panturle, completely taken aback.

He took off his trousers and also his shirt.

"Must enjoy it," he said.

He got into the sheets carefully, one leg after the other.

"It's coarse like fresh sand," he said, "and it all smells of lavender. Be quick, Arsule, if you want some of it, or I'll use up the freshness of the sheets and they'll be all crumpled for you."

Once when Panturle, who had been lopping the cypress, put down his bundle in front of the hearth, she said: "No, you really ought to put the wood in the stables. When it's here I've got to sweep it up, and it makes my back ache. Go on. Just put it out there." He took it out and the matter was settled for good.

Another time, early one morning in midsummer, she had the Gaudissart stream blocked with branches and mud. She placed a sheet in the bed of the stream and fastened it down well at the bottom with stones. She thus made a sort of clear basin. Then she had a bath. She washed herself down with a handful of soapwort. That evening when they were in bed her skin had the lustre of gold. She said to him: "Leave me alone. You smell of mildewed salt." She said this jokingly, but the next day Panturle went into the stream. He, of course, did not need a sheet.

The same sort of thing happened time and again.

Then both of them became troubled without knowing why, so troubled that they found the mornings bitter. It was in the air. It filled them with bitterness. It was particularly noticeable after Panturle had been hunting. Especially after he had left on the table a strangled rabbit, as stiff as a root, or a quail crushed by a trap.

At such times neither Panturle nor Arsule said a word.

One day, when they had had quite enough of this meat, Arsule simply put a large quantity of potatoes to boil and nothing else. And that was all she put on the plates. Panturle looked at the potatoes, at the rabbit strung up to the ceiling in a towel, at the blood on the towel, and at the flies. He looked at Arsule.

"I'll tell you what I'm thinking about," he said. "It's that by sharpening and putting a good handle on the blade that's in the loft, I could make a good spade of it. On the sunny side of the slope by Reine-Porque there's a fine bit of ground and I think, if I fired the broom, it would grow anything we wanted. I also think I might be able to make a plough . . . ."

"Well, that would be fine," Arsule replied.

"Here's your clean shirt and here's another pair of trousers. Do you want your jacket?"

"No, it's hot," he replied. "What I really need is a sack, because if things go all right over there I'll take the grain right away. It's higher up here and sowing can begin earlier. Give me Caroline too; I'm going to find a billygoat for her."

Caroline seemed sad, standing there before the broad daylight of the doorway. She did not dare to come out of the shade of the stables. She blinked. She was lean. She had hollow sides. The flies made the skin of her belly tremble.

"Biquette, Biquette," called Panturle, and he made the gesture with his hands of giving her some grass. "Here, here." She did not move. She stood there against the glare as if in front of a wall.

Arsule persuaded her by imitating with her lips the sound of a kiss. She came out and advanced stiffly. She seemed to look beyond things as men do when they are in a dream. She came and placed her head against the woman's belly. She rubbed her sides against Arsule's sides. A good while. Quite long. Until Arsule said: "Go along, Nanny."

She gave the chain to Panturle and Caroline followed him.

It was the beginning of the afternoon and nice and warm, despite the first round clouds passing by trailing their shadows. They were sea clouds. They rose and their shadows followed them like footprints.

The wood was all flecked with yellow. From Reine-Porque one looked down on things; Cat's Vale and the lowland were like an old iron cauldron that has been badly cleaned and is rusting. The top of the sky alone was alive with that regular flight of clouds. Below, near the ground, the air was motionless. It hung round the hills and the trees, warm and heavy, like damp wool.

Right at the bottom of Cat's Vale a slight mist slept on the trees, like a small surface of milk at the bottom of the cauldron. When one bent over the hollow, one noticed a smell of mushrooms and of decaying wood.

A magpie had just left a branch of the poplar. With a skilful wing she dived into the dull green shadows of the undergrowth. Two dead leaves left the branch after her and fell.

"Have you finished your game, Caroline?" Panturle asked the goat, which continued to pull to the left to browse off a burdock.

Panturle took the paths that only he knew.

That way he came upon L'Amoureux's farm, all of a sudden, on turning round a bend in the vale at the edge of the clayey lands. Pulling the goat, he soon reached the shade of the plane trees and found himself among people. It made a queer impression on him. Over there was a man ploughing – a small man and a small horse; there was a man crossing the fallow land and there a man bending down watering a whetstone for sharpening sickles; a woman drawing water from the well; another hanging out washing on a line; a man stretching himself like a cat at the granary door and another scraping a spade . . . . L'Amoureux was beneath the plane trees in front of the farm. He was about to take his scythe hanging on the big branch. He stopped short and remained with his arm in the air. He watched the man arriving with a goat.

"Well, I never! If that's not a surprise! Why, Panturle, I thought you were dead!"

"I've no wish to be."

"Well, I never!"

L'Amoureux's arm fell on Panturle's shoulder.

"It's me, right enough," said Panturle.

"Real earnest," L'Amoureux continued. "I thought so. Alphonsine, come and look! Alphonsine!"

She was hanging out washing and looking at the two men from between the linen. As she hurried towards them, her big, flabby bosom shaking up and down, she dried her hands on her apron.

She could not get over it, either.

"It's true. We were speaking about you only a short time ago. Well, you must come and have a drink!"

As it wasn't to be refused, she went into the kitchen and they

74

heard her opening the cupboard. She came to the doorstep, holding the bottle up to her eyes.

"It's not that. Wait a minute."

"And mind you fetch us the right one."

Finally she brought out the right one: a liqueur of hyssop, which can be watered if one likes, but which men drink neat.

"Hey, boys!" L'Amoureux called out.

The three farm labourers standing near by, who had already seen the bottle out of the corner of their eyes, approached.

They had their glasses. They all drank one another's health. Alphonsine thought of the women.

"Tiennette, come along too and bring yourself a glass."

"So here's to your health," said Etiennette, who was late and drank to everybody alone.

"This is Panturle," said L'Amoureux. "There! That's a man who'd suit you fine!"

"She might do worse," said Clodomir, laughing. She was his girl.

Etiennette bowed her head, which was like a red apple. She giggled and looked at Clodomir through her eyelashes. Clodomir stroked his light yellow moustache with the tip of his first finger and watched her out of the corner of his eye with an amused look.

"Well, where were you going like that?"

"Just here."

"That's all right, then."

"It's like this. First of all, it's for her." He pointed to Caroline, rubbing her muzzle against him. "Have you a he-goat or do you know of one? She can't remain like that any longer. It's undermining her. And then, for us . . ."

"Well, there's always Turcan's billygoat. Leave her here. I'll get Etiennette to take her along tomorrow."

"And then?"

"Wait a bit."

L'Amoureux turned to Clodomir.

"And you'd better sharpen the two scythes," he said.

The man understood and got up.

"You understand. I prefer just the two of us talking man to man. One never knows. You know servants have a way of catching onto a dozen words here and there, about things they've heard and that gives them a dozen stones to throw at your face afterwards. Go on."

"Well, I'd like to ask you for some wheat seed. I'd like to grow a bit. I can't pay you now, but I'd give it back to you at harvest time. And then, in a little while, when it's convenient, I'd like you to lend me your horse one day. I'd pay that as you like, either in money or wheat."

L'Amoureux considered awhile.

"That can be managed," he said finally. "How much wheat do you want?"

"Give me three hundred kilos to begin with, if it'll be all right."

"Right."

"Send them up to me tomorrow morning, as far as Reine-Porque. The cart can get there. I'll manage from there."

"Right. And the horse?"

"That's as you like, when it's free."

"Well, you can fetch it . . . in three days."

"Right. You're doing me a real good turn, L'Amoureux."

"Have you seen the children?" Alphonsine asked.

"They were here a minute or two ago."

"Tiennette, have you seen the children?"

"No, ma'am."

"Well, where can they be?"

She immediately cast a severe glance round about her. There was the ditch; there was the well; there were the big fox traps all set even in broad daylight.

"Nano! Nano! Nano!"

"Lison!" cried the father.

A moment of silence. All three listened. But finally the little ones replied:

"Yeth . . . ."

At the same time they emerged from the grass that hid them. The first-born, Jean, led his sister Elise by the hand. In their other hands they held, like a candle, a big chalice of meadow-saffron.

"Hurt m'self," the little girl said immediately, fearing a smack.

Alphonsine met the two children with a big loaf of bread. She was also fumbling in the pocket of her apron.

"Here."

The little girl held out her hand and received three dried figs and two nuts.

"Here."

She turned to the little boy, who had his hand out, and he received his three figs and two nuts.

"Wait a minute."

She cut the bread with a big knife which looked like a bill-hook. She bent over the loaf and held it between her bosom and her stomach, and she cut slowly without making crumbs.

Panturle watched the good bread. It was big and solid. It was bread of the fields, bread of flour ground with a marble mortar. It was a russet bread from which a long, straight, and flashing straw, like a sunbeam, might sometimes be drawn.

All of a sudden he saw what he would do, what he would re-create, what he had already begun to do by arriving there. He understood that anxiety which they had felt, that shadow in Arsule who was usually as lovely as water. It would disappear. It was sure now. He had understood. It would disappear once they had placed on the table up there at Aubignane, in the last house, the loaf of bread, warm and heavy, bread which they would have made themselves, the three of them together: he, Arsule, and the earth.

All of a sudden, as Alphonsine turned round and was taking the bread away, he sprang forward and cried:

"Alphonsine!"

He immediately felt a little ashamed as soon as she returned with her bread.

"You'll be surprised, but I was going to ask you something. I can't pay you for it, so I'll owe it to you. It's not for me," he added, for he saw that she was already handing it to him and that L'Amoureux was saying: "Bring some olives, too." "It's not for me," he repeated.

"I'll tell you because it'll get known, and anyhow, well, it's right I should say so: I have a woman up there with me and it'll please her."

"Take the lot, then," said Alphonsine.

To see that they gave him the lot pained him. It made him blink as if he were eating laurels.

"I'll pay it back to you."

"You can do that if you want us to be angry."

He did not want to share the four o'clock snack at their table.

"I've still got to go to Jasmin's place."

But he asked them to give him twenty kilograms of wheat seed right away so as to be able to show it to Arsule that evening, that she should know at once that things had begun and were well in hand.

And he started back with the loaf under his arm and the sack on his shoulder.

Lanky Belline was in the yard counting her ducks. She was thin as a cypress and nearly as tall. She wore a sky-blue working jacket.

Here the country had already changed. It had something below the surface. Water oozed out. There was a fine meadow and willows. There was an orchard. There was an enormous birch which seemed like foam as soon as the wind touched it. There was a fountain. There was a good, solid fence that surrounded it all. It seemed to be all tree and grass, swollen with as much water as anyone could wish for.

Panturle came up to the fence.

"Hey, Belline!"

She turned her long horse's face towards him.

"Do you remember me?"

"Yes."

She made no sign towards the latch of the gate. She merely brought all her ducks under the protection of her eyes. One could understand her feeling. He said:

"I should like to see old Gaubert."

"He's in there."

She pointed to the house. She added nothing. She picked up a big snail and called to a duck which seemed to be navigating in bad weather across the meadow.

That was all right. Panturle waited a moment and then went off to the house.

Old Gaubert was near the stove. He was sitting in a straight-backed chair. His hands were resting on his stick. His head was resting on his hands.

He said: "Oh!" when he saw Panturle, then he spent a while trying to raise his head. Finally he succeeded. Panturle laughed and held out his hand to him.

"Oh, Father Gaubert, it's a long time since we last saw each other. And are you comfortable like that, near the stove? Ah, you old scoundrel, you've found the best kind of work to do now!"

But Gaubert's hands remained on his stick. They trembled. With a great effort he turned his head and raised his eyes up to Panturle's eyes.

"You take my hand from there. Take it. Please do. I can't hold it out."

At a bound he put down his sack and his loaf and took hold of that hand which was like wet linen between his good, solid hands.

"Well, now, Gaubert. You don't mean to say … ? Well, now!"

The hands were soft and dead and the arms were dead. Panturle touched them and they were like lifeless rope. In Gaubert's eyes there was the look of an animal caught in a trap. And now, from nearer at hand, he smelt of urine.

"Well, yes, you see. It's like that."

"When did it happen to you?"

"One morning something got unknotted under my kidneys. Belline said: 'That's all nonsense. Try!' I tried. Nothing to be done. It had got me."

Panturle remained there holding Gaubert's dead hands. He was bending over him and looking into his eyes. He wanted to put a bit of strength into those hands.

"And what did Jasmin say?"

"Nothing."

Panturle could not get over that disappearance of strength from a man like Gaubert who had always worked and who now sat there like a log. Gaubert was the first to speak again.

"Well, how are things that you should wander as far as here?"

Panturle no longer dared say, but it was a thing he had so much wanted. He had thought of that plough so much all day.

"It's like this: I've come . . . I came . . . to see you and I said to myself: 'Perhaps he'd like to take up his work again a bit.' You see, I didn't know. So I came to say: 'Make me a plough.' But . . . "

"Oh, of course . . . ."

For a while nothing else could be heard than the clock counting its seeds: tick-tick. The sun had succeeded in passing through the orchard. A beam crossed the pane and broke up in a pail of water.

"That hardly seems to be like you," Gaubert said. "You were always more of a hunter. A sabre would be more in your line."

"Hunting's too variable from day to day. All said and done, it's not real work. And then there's never anything else than meat. I've found some land on the other side of the knoll. You know where I mean. It seems to be deep and rich. I've been feeling like growing some wheat."

"It's funny that you should be taken that way now."

"It's that I'm no longer alone. I've a wife. A family can't live on game. Since she came, I need bread, and she too. So . . . "

"That's natural, and it's a good sign."

"Oh, but what's the matter, Gaubert, old man? You're crying? What are they doing to you? It's Belline, isn't it? Would you like me to talk to Jasmin? Tell me. What's the matter?"

If Gaubert had had his hands free, he would have hidden those three tears which brimmed over his eyes. But his hands were nailed to his stick and he could not hide his face. So he remained there with his head erect and tears falling from his desperate eyes.

After a while, during which Panturle did not dare to speak, Gaubert sniffed up his tears like a little child.

"No, it wasn't Belline this time. I just couldn't help it. It's because I see that the earth at Aubignane is going to start off again. Wanting bread, and the woman, that's it. It's a good sign. I know that. There's no mistaking it. It'll start off again with a good spurt and it will become man's earth once more. But who will be up there at my forge?"

"Ah, Gaubert, that's not for an old man to think about. You mustn't cry about that. You know quite well that one day you would have to make way for another. That's fate. The only thing to be sorry about is that the man who'll come there won't be able to make ploughs like you. But you've won your decorations now. You've wrought iron long enough. Your lot now is the orchard and shade and your son's house . . . ."

"Now you're talking to me in the same familiar way as you used to."

"Yes."

"Why?"

"I don't know."

"Let's suppose you don't know," he retorted, "but all the same it shows that you have understood why I was crying. My lot is to be here in my chair like a scarecrow in a fig tree, not being able to move a finger even to chase off the flies. And when I'm in a place where I'm in the way because they want to cook or to sweep, Jasmin takes the chair on one side, Belline takes it on the other, and they carry me like a piece of furniture. Oh! At first when I was here, my lot was the shade and the orchard and my son's house and the baby. I taught the magpies to talk for it by keeping them under a flower-pot. I used to play pranks. It was fun. Now I'm being punished. I ought not to have left the village . . . . And Mamèche!" he resumed.

"She left one fine morning. That's all I know."

"Yes? Well, it's something that must have trimmed the old wood. It'll start off again."

They remained silent thus for a long while, penetrating to the depths of each other's thoughts. Then Gaubert said:

"Panturle, I'll make you that plough, or it'll be nearly the same thing. I want it to be one of mine that starts things off. Listen! You'll see. Just look first and make sure that Belline's still in the orchard."

"Yes, she's at the other end, over there, near the plum trees."

"That's all right. Pass the broomstick under the cupboard. There. Do you feel anything hard? Pull."

It was a ploughshare.

It was a ploughshare! A ploughshare as bare as a knife. A ploughshare that was obstinate, sharp, and arrogant, with the hollow flank of an animal that races across the hills, a fine smooth skin. One could balance it on one's fist.

Gaubert whistled through his teeth: " ... of a bitch. He's of a good stock, he is. Yes, of a good stock. It's the last one. I made him while I was still at Aubignane. Take him. Put him in your sack. If Belline came in, there'd be the devil to pay. Put it in your sack and then listen. For the ploughshare's a lot, but it's not everything . . . . You must go to the forge up there. You know that towards the last I slept below, near the smithy. In that place there's a cupboard, a big cupboard. Open it. Here, now, take the key, here in my vest pocket. Take the key. Afterwards you can throw it away. It won't be of any more use. There in the cupboard you'll find the wood of a swing-plough all ready, all finished and twisted in the right way. Wood of good stock, too, the wood that's needed for this ploughshare. You'll fix the ploughshare with the screws and the bolts that are also in the cupboard, folded in a piece of newspaper. Now, if it's to plough there where you mentioned, on the hill behind the village, there where it's hard, you'll have to twist the wood a bit more – not too much, a bit, just a bit bent, like a coffee spoon. You see? For that you'll have to soak the wood for three days in the cypress hole. Three days, not more, and twist slowly, pressing on your thigh, but first try the plough as it is. I'd prefer you didn't touch it."

Panturle looked at the fine ploughshare.

"No," he said, I don't want to ruin it all! You say that the bolts are in the paper? I'll leave it as it is. It'll go as you made it. If it needs forcing a bit, I'll force it, but I'll leave it as it is. What I want is wheat, wheat growing all over Chènevières hillock, wheat growing at Aubignane right up to the houses. I want to fill the whole place with wheat, as much as the earth'll bear."

Gaubert remained motionless in his chair with his dead hands crossed on his stick. He made an effort with his head.

"It can bear it, all right, our earth. Believe me, it can bear a good covering. In my time it was famed for it. The day that a strong man puts his back into it, there'll be a blessing of wheat . . . ."

Belline entered by the back door. She had a duck under her arm and was stroking its feathers.

"Second childhood," she said.

It was night when Panturle returned. The door was shut. He knocked with his fist.

"Who's there?" asked Arsule's voice.

"Me."

She opened.

"I was beginning to grow restless, you know."

He put down his sack of wheat on the table.

"Look," he said. "Look, I haven't wasted my time. And that, look at that!"

He held up against the light of the hearth the fine ploughshare bare as a knife.

"Oh," she said, "that's lovely! It looks like the prow of a ship."

II

THEY WENT TO FETCH THE WHEAT. L'AMOUREUX was waiting for them at Reine-Porque. The sacks had been unloaded near the fountain.

"You see," he said to L'Amoureux, "this is my wife."

And to Arsule:

"That, you see, that's a real, good friend!"

"You'll have to come to our place, one day," L'Amoureux said. "Alphonsine would be glad."

And he went off again with his cart.

There were six big sacks of wheat near the fountain.

Panturle heaved one onto his back.

"I'll go and come back. You'll look after the sacks in the meantime."

He did it like that to the last sack. When he put it on his shoulder, he said:

"We've earned our day. Let's go back by the plateau. I've had enough of going up and down."

There had been a sharp, heavy downpour the night before. It had crushed the wood. Leaves had fallen. On the plateau the grass had been crushed too. It lay in whorls in all directions.

"Winter's coming on," said Arsule.

She followed Panturle. They were on the edge of that plateau where at the same time she had been so frightened and so hot with love. She thought of it. She thought that it was the wind that had married her. Her life had only started there. All that had happened before scarcely counted any more. She thought of it from time to time as of a disease from which she had been cured. And when she thought of it, she immediately felt the need of looking at Panturle. She lived peacefully at last, and clearly her life was filled with joy.

It was the plateau where all night long the rain had ridden rough-shod over the grass.

All of a sudden Panturle stopped and threw down his sack. With his arms stretched out, he barred the road and held Arsule behind him.

"Stay there."

He went forward three steps in the grass and looked at his feet.

He seemed to be reflecting. He came back, picked up his sack, took Arsule by the arm, and drew her across the grass by another way.

For the rest of the day he remained quite strange and anxious. He could not make up his mind about anything. He measured out the grain, but it was quite clear that his thoughts were elsewhere. Then he left everything and went away. He went up to the village. He weighed his shoulders against the door at Mamèche's house. The door fell flat on the floor and he entered.

He tried to unfold the sheets which were on the table. They were in shreds. What with rats and other animals, they had been properly messed up.

He went down to the house again by the fields at the back, and took advantage of Arsule's being down at the water to go in quickly, quickly. He searched in the kneading-trough and in the cupboards.

He ferreted around. He asked himself: "Where does she put them?"

Finally, tired of looking, he went to their bed, which was made. He undid it with a sweeping backward movement of his hand. He took the sheet in which he and Arsule slept. As Arsule came in downstairs he jumped out of the window with the sheet rolled under his arm.

He went out on the plateau. Then he came back with something folded in the sheet. A little package, like a bundle of short twigs, well dried, because it crackled, and something round on top which wobbled like a watermelon and which tended to slip. Round that he wound the sheet four or five times.

He came to the communal well. And he had to push his big body through the thorns before reaching the lip of the well. He knotted the bundle. He also knotted two big stones in the package. He looked down below at the black water, which shone like new iron.

Then he threw in the bundle and watched until the water had eaten it all up.

He remained there a good while bending over the well and said to himself aloud:

"Yes, it's certainly here that she would have wanted it."

That evening he sat down on the hearthstone and started talking.

"There's one person from here who'd have been pleased to see us together."

"Who's that?" asked Arsule.

"A woman from here. They called her Mamèche. She kept on saying to me: 'Take a wife. Take one.' She even said: 'And if you like, I'll go and find you one!' So much so, that she must have left for that."

At that Arsule had nothing to reply except to purse her lips a bit.

"So much so, that she must have left for that and died."

After that he had to tell about the sheet torn off the bed and everything. Arsule had sat down next to Panturle and had nestled up to him, because death, when spoken about, is a thing that freezes one up. Then she started thinking.

"On the plateau, you said?"

"Yes."

"Was she very dark when she was alive, with something not clear in her movements?"

"Yes," Panturle answered in astonishment.

"Yes. I'll tell you. Then it was me she went to fetch. If we passed by Aubignane this spring, it was because something forced us towards here, out of our way, through fear. It was she who appeared in the grass. She forced me to come here. I don't regret it, but it's the honest truth."

She told Panturle everything, little by little. Everything from the beginning to the end, and then he smiled slightly, for he understood how things had linked up.

"That's all right."

He turned his head and looked at the wheat measured out.

For three days it was as if on board a ship. No respite. All the time doing something. The first day, the whole time, it was either: "Arsule, give me the screwdriver," or: "Arsule, while rummaging about, did you come across a box like this with tools in it?"

Then, finally, towards evening, he cried: "Arsule, come and see!" There in front of the house in the fresh grass, standing in the meadow like a grasshopper, was the plough, all ready.

"With that . . . " said Panturle.

The next day they burned the grass on the field. They had to watch that it did not spread too far.

The day after, and the night after, right until dawn there were almost the noises of a real farm, and Panturle was unable to sleep.

There was the horse, down below in the stables. They had put him there in Caroline's place. They heard him stamp, shake the chain, scratch himself on the wagon shafts, and even neigh tremblingly like a trumpet, because he was a stallion and mistook the smell of the goat for the smell of a mare.

By dint of looking towards the window in the room filled with night, he saw the dawn the other side of the pane. It lighted up all of a sudden. It was pink, which meant it would be fine. Panturle got up and Arsule, who seemed to be sleeping with her nose towards the wall, turned and said:

"I'm going too. I want to see."

"Wait a bit. With that mad horse, as soon as he smells a woman near him, he goes crazy. I'll harness him. You'll go down there later on."

There, now it was going to begin.

He had the line drawn straight to the bushes over there which he left on purpose as a landmark, and others would lean against it. And when, from here till over yonder by the young cedar it would be all covered, when it would be like a roof of tiles, then it would be all right. Forward!

His animal-killer's instinct helped him plunge the sharp coulter briskly into the earth. It groaned; it gave way. The steel tore a good piece, which opened up black and rich. And with one stroke the earth pulled itself together. It fought and seemed to bite to defend itself. The whole harness was shaken by it, right from the horse's jaw to Panturle's shoulders. He immediately looked at the plough-share. It was whole and yet they had hit a nasty rock.

"You shall pass through all the same," said Panturle with his teeth clenched.

Now the big blade, which resembled the front of a ship, navigated in a calmed earth.

"Now, Nègre, pull away, you lazy devil!"

It all went joyfully and easily. There was the sun, which had jumped over the hills and was rising. And there was Arsule, who had jumped over the stream and was coming up to him.

III

MICHEL'S COACH NOW STOPPED AT THE FOOT OF Vachères heights at ten o'clock. He had found a way of doing it. Nobody knew how he did it, but the fact remained that it was ten o'clock.

"We'll wait for old Valigrane."

Michel began to sound his horn. They had stopped under the shadow of the high-steepled church which was overgrown with ivy. There came Valigrane, hurrying down the road like a lad; he even took the short cuts at the turns. He hurried. In fact he hurried so much that he looked as if he would fall.

"Hey! Don't hurry! We've plenty of time. The house is not on fire!"

"I didn't want to keep you waiting."

"That's all right, we're happy enough here, in the shade."

Valigrane mopped his bald head with a big, clean handkerchief.

"Will you get inside or sit by me?" Michel asked, pointing to the seat near him on the box.

"I'll sit by you, in the fresh air. I don't like being shut up inside there."

The horses had now begun to go up the slow, winding slope, making all the collar-bells tinkle. It was hot, for it was August.

Michel, who knew why Valigrane was going to Banon, said:

"There'll be a lot of people."

"Yes, that's what I was saying to the wife. It's just on the day of the fair."

"It's awkward for them, but with this hot weather, they couldn't keep him a day longer. It was impossible. He'd already begun to smell. I told them plainly: 'You needn't even close.' They've a back door. There's no point in closing the café on the very day when there's business. The hearse will arrive at the back, they'll load it, and go off. Nobody'll see anything in front. That's right, isn't it?"

"Oh, for that matter! . . . It is a nuisance, just on the day when they're by way of earning a good hundred or hundred and fifty francs – it doesn't happen so often – to have to close and send the customers to others. He's had enough bad luck as it is . . . "

"That's what I said."

"That's what he'd say, if he could still speak: 'Carry on, and no fuss.' He was all the same a decent fellow, was Uncle Joseph."

They arrived at a turning from where they could see the whole country below. It was not golden with wheat as usual, but only a dirty yellow, and the earth could be seen through the yellow.

"Oh, what a year!"

"Is it the same at your place?"

"Yes. As a rule we have fifty loads, but this year we may not even have five, and poor at that, with ten times more work, and harder than usual. So, you see . . . "

"Yes. It's the same everywhere."

"You're right. It's the same at Reillanne, Forcalquier, and Manosque. People wanted to sow that corn. It was a new stunt again, and that's what's happened now."

"Besides, there was the great storm."

"Yes, of course, and what a distance it covered!"

"And what damage it did!"

"Yes, it did a lot of damage," old Valigrane said, after revolving in his mind his memories of wheat-fields, "and it's all because of the craze."

"When that sort of thing is allowed to meddle with people's lives, it makes a good number of idiots, but when it interferes with plants and things connected with plants . . . "

"I'll tell you something: I myself went to a place – I won't tell you where, you'd know who I'm talking about. There was a man who was supposed to know something about farming, or at any rate people said so. He was a professor, you know, a man paid by the government. He had rented a small farm. It was smart, in good order, quite sound, and had good regular ground. There were vines, mulberry trees, a meadow, and cherry trees . . . you see? Well, this professor got going. He certainly got going properly. He took off his coat and his vest, rolled up his shirt-sleeves and got to work. After a year the place was a desert. A desert, I tell you. All the trees fell ill . . . it was upsetting to see them. No more cherries, no more vines, no more meadow. It all seemed to be disgusted with life. There was a bit of something here and a bit of something else there, and such and such a branch had to turn that way . . . . He put the grapes into little paper bags – yes, it was like that. If you had thought of taking over the farm, you wouldn't touch it now, even if they made you a present of it: it's all dead. You see the sort of man, the root doctor, with his big book in his hand? You can't learn all that in books!"

"You've always got a new story."

"No, this is what I mean: you spoke about the storm. Well, if they'd sown wheat from our parts, wheat accustomed to the whims of our earth and our seasons, it might perhaps have resisted. You know, the storm flattens down the wheat. Well, that happens once. You mustn't think that a plant doesn't reason. It says to itself: 'All right! I'll have to stiffen up a bit,' and, little by little it hardens its stem and finally it keeps standing in spite of the storms. It manages to get weathered. But if you go and fetch things from the other end of the world, if you go and listen to those fine gentlemen with their books: 'Sow some of this, sow some of that; ah, don't do that!' well, damn it, that's what happens to you!"

"Sure, I'm of your opinion, Valigrane."

"Of course, we all get caught. As for me, my son wanted it, my son-in-law wanted it. 'You want that sort of corn?' I said. 'All right, we'll have it, then!' And now they look like fools in front of the barns. Now they understand, but only now! There's plenty of room for the mistral to fool around in the empty barns. That's the situation! If at least it had taught them a lesson!"

The road was now sloping more gently uphill. They could already see the edge of the wood up there, and the dry grass of the plateau.

"What's the matter with your grey horse?"

The horse on the left turned his head towards the valley which pierced the wood. He shook his withers and stretched out his neck, neighing away towards something in the distance.

"Ah! It's taken him again; let him amuse himself. Don't you know how it came upon him? It was about the month of May . . . . From here, you know, one can see Aubignane hill. Look, it's over there. We were going up like this, when he started neighing. I didn't take much notice of it that time. The next day, it was the same thing, and again the day after, and always at the same place. And he always looked round the same way. I said to myself: 'What on earth can there be over there?' I looked. Up there, at Aubignane, where it was usually reddish like corn, it was green, covered with green, and a fine deep green too. He had noticed it, that animal!"

"They do notice things . . . "

"Yes."

Now they were on the plateau. The horses began trotting again, and the air was less hot.

"There . . . you can see," said Michel, "it's the same everywhere."

He pointed with his whip at the stubble between the grass, with small stooks of corn about the size of molehills.

In spite of the bad crops, the big summer market had filled up the little town. There were men and carts on all the roads, women with bundles, children in their Sunday clothes, holding tightly in their right hands their ten-sou piece to buy doughnuts. They came down from all the hills. There was a large group on the road from Ongles, all packed together, with the carts rolling slowly and everybody in the dust. There were people on foot, with bags on their shoulders and goats behind them that looked as small as seeds on the paths away over near Laroche. There were others taking a rest under the poplars on the road from Simiane, right under the walls, in the midst of the clangour of all the midday bells. There were still others who had stopped at the crossways of the mill. People from Laroche had met people from the Buëch. They had become intermingled like a bundle of branches in the midst of a stream. They took short glances at one another, which went straight from their eyes to their sacks of wheat. They immediately understood one another.

"Ah, what bad times we're going through!"

"And how light the grain is!"

"And how little there is!"

"Ah, yes!"

The women were thinking that up there on the market place there were cloth merchants, with dresses and ribbons, and that they would have to pass by their stalls, and do without. From where they were, they could already smell the waffles frying; they could hear faint sounds trickling from the barrel-organs and the merry-go-rounds. Those invitations to the fair in that fine, sunny atmosphere seemed to reproach them for their bad wheat and made them feel glum.

In the sloping meadow, under the shade of apple trees, farm folk were sitting at their meal. Usually they went to the inn, to eat beef stew. Today they had to be careful of their money.

Not that the inn was empty. Oh, no! There was no more room at the long table in the middle, and they had already put small tables at the sides, between the windows, and the two maids were so flushed that they appeared to have ripe tomatoes under their hair. They ran from the kitchen to the dining-room without stopping, and the brown sauce kept spilling over their arms. It was not that the inn people usually had time to spare to tell their beads, but the customers that day were mainly grain-brokers from the lower country, big-bellied men who had come there to skin the poor country people, because they could use their tongues to better purpose and wanted to buy as cheaply as possible. They weren't much of a crowd. On the square, pedlars and packmen had put up their canvas booths between the lime trees. Everything was lying about in confusion under the tents: hats, slippers, shoes, coats, heavy corduroy trousers, children's dolls, girls' coral necklaces, saucepans and steam-cookers for housewives, playthings and tassels for the little ones, nipples for sucklings who do not want to be weaned. It was very convenient. There were cloth merchants, selling piece-goods, with their wooden yardsticks just a little too short.

"And I'll give good measure. Step this way!"

There were sweets-stalls, and lollipop sellers, and fish-stalls, with youngsters clinging to them like flies to a pot of honey. There was the man who sold herb-tea and little booklets where all the ills of the body were explained and cures given. Near the weighing-pen there was a many-coloured merry-go-round, rumbling round amidst the trees like a bumble-bee.

The noise and cries which rose in the heat were enough to deafen you and make you feel you had water in your ears. At Agathange's they'd left the doors of the café open. A stream of smoke and shouts flowed out. Inside, there were people who had dined on sausage and white wine at marble-topped tables, and who were now arguing in their loud voices, shoving the empty glasses about with their fists. Agathange was tired out. He had been on his feet since morning. He had not had a minute to sit down. Always on the go from the kitchen to the café, in and out among the tables and between the chairs. There was a man there at the end of the room calling for a vermouth. He would have to go down to the cellar. He was in his shirt-sleeves. It was a fine shirt with red flowers. He wore his best trousers, and no collar. The celluloid collar was lying ready on the kitchen table by the clean cups. There were also two iron studs and a ready-made tie, which was black and new, and specially bought for the impending ceremony.

The door of the passage was at the far end of the kitchen, which opened on the staircase leading up to the bedrooms. It was ajar. It gave the impression of being painted with the light of a candle, which shone from above. Between whiles, when there was a breathing space, Agathange went to the door and called gently:

"Norine, do you need anything?"

A weak voice came down:

"No."

"Not a drop of rum? Do take a little rum."

"No, I'm all right, carry on with the work."

While serving, Agathange kept an eye on the clock. It would soon be three o'clock.

"Four brandies? All right."

It would soon be three o'clock. And here was Norine, who had come down into the kitchen.

"I suppose you thought of the coffin, didn't you?"

She asked Agathange because they had not yet come.

It was high time. With the heat it would be much better if he were inside.

Agathange was carrying the bottle of brandy under his arm and the coffee-pot in his hand; on the other hand, the tray with some cups.

"Yes, Aunt, I already told you I remembered it, but think of it, just the day of the fair. Anyhow, it's not yet time – not quite – it's not yet three. He told me he'd come and put him in at three. It's five to. Listen, it's striking three. He'll come, all right, you needn't worry."

The little old woman looked at the clean cuffs on the table, the collar, the black tie, at Agathange, who was red and shiny with sweat, and at the cash-drawer, wide open and overbrimming with five-franc notes . . . .

"It's not that I'm worrying, but he's beginning to smell rather badly, you know . . . ."

It was Jérémie who pushed aside the curtain door, crying:

"Monsieur Astruc, do you want some wheat?"

Monsieur Astruc was so taken aback by the question that he turned round bodily, making the table and glasses shake.

"Where the devil have you seen any, man? There's not a handful of decent wheat in your whole countryside."

"I don't know whether there ain't a handful of decent grain, but I've seen six sacks full, for sure, and good at that, I can tell you."

He came in and walked with his long legs up to the table. Monsieur Astruc looked at him. Jérémie knew what a look meant.

"Give me a cigarette."

Monsieur Astruc brought out his pack.

"I'll take two by your leave."

"Well, then?"

"Well, it's over there, behind the roundabouts, at the place where the mules are usually hitched up. It needed me to have a look over there. There's a fellow there with his sacks in front of him. He hasn't spoken to anybody. He just looks around. He's there, waiting. I say to him:

"'Hey, man, what have you got there?'

"'Wheat,' he says. And the funny part about it is that it's true. You know, Monsieur Astruc, that when I see a thing I know it. You know that, and it's not the first time . . . . Well, I'm sure that you've never seen wheat like that."

"Give me a light."

"What will you drink?"

"Nothing. I've had enough. But if you strike the bargain, you'll give me something. I could as well have gone to see old Jacques, but I thought of you first."

Monsieur Astruc had a comfortable belly, well folded in a double-breasted waistcoat, with a watch-chain tying it all together, and all this was planted on two little legs. He got up suddenly.

"I must go and see. Agathange, I'm coming back; have some beers served."

There were six sacks, all right. They could be seen from a distance. Monsieur Astruc had already counted them. He had already noticed that people were looking at the wheat. He had already noticed that the other brokers had not yet arrived.

"Let me pass, let me pass!"

His first glance was at the wheat. He gasped at it.

"My word!"

It was as heavy as small shot. It was healthy and golden, and cleaner than anything that could be found nowadays; not a single husk. Nothing but grain: dry, solid, and clean as water from a stream. He wanted to touch it, to feel it flowing between his fingers. It was not an everyday sight.

"Don't touch it!" said the man.

Monsieur Astruc looked at him.

"Don't touch it. If you want to buy it, then it's all right. But if it's just to look, then look with your eyes."

It was for buying, but he didn't touch it. He understood. He would do the same himself.

"Where did you grow that?"

"At Aubignane."

Monsieur Astruc again bent over the fine grain. Everybody could see it, free of straw and dust, filling out the canvas sack. He said nothing, and nobody spoke, not even the fellow behind the sacks who was the vender. There was nothing to say. It was fine wheat, and everybody knew it.

"It's not machine-threshed, is it?"

"It's threshed with that," said the man.

He showed his large hands, bruised by the flail, and as he opened them it made the scabs crack and bleed. Near the man stood a small young woman, rather pretty, all brick-coloured from the sun. She was looking contentedly at the man from head to foot. She said to him:

"Shut your hand, it's bleeding."

He shut his hand.

"Well?"

"Well, I'll take it. Is it all you have?"

"Yes. I've four sacks more, but they're for myself."

"What do you want to do with them?"

"Bread, of course."

"Give them to me. I'll buy them too."

"No, I told you I'm keeping them."

"I'll give you a hundred and ten francs."

"Not more?" asked a man who stood there.

The fellow behind the sacks glanced at the small woman. He smiled with his eyes and lips, then he turned towards Monsieur Astruc, without smiling, with the same look as he had a moment before when he said: "Don't touch it."

"I don't know whether it ought to be more or less, but I want a hundred and thirty."

Monsieur Astruc looked down at the wheat. Then he said:

"All right, I'll take it!"

He did not speak the words but shouted them, because the organ of the merry-go-rounds had begun to rumble.

"But the ten sacks!" he shouted again.

"No," answered the man. "These six and no more. I'm keeping the others, I tell you. My wife likes good bread."

What a deal that wheat was! Everybody talked about it. First of all, Monsieur Astruc put two big handfuls in his pocket, and he showed them, here and there and everywhere.

"Have a look," he would say.

And he would open his fat hand, full of that beautiful wheat which was as fine and solid as a man.

"My word!" the people would say. "And this year, especially!"

"Any year, you can say," Monsieur Astruc would add, "any year! Why, it's prize wheat. It's the first time I've seen anything like it. And all threshed with a flail and winnowed by the mistral. The man who did that's no sluggard. His hands are bleeding from it."

The people would listen and whistle a long whistle of admiration.

"Well, I'm damned!"

And Jérémie!

He went about the fair.

"Have you seen that wheat Astruc bought?"

When people said "Yes," he added:

"It was me who found it. He was going away empty-handed without doing a bit of business. It was me who found it."

If he were contradicted he would catch the man by the shoulder and shout:

99

"Go and see it, then! You'll never again see the like of it!"

What excitement it caused!

By four o'clock in the afternoon, people were talking about nothing else.

"It's a man from Aubignane, I'm told."

"I think I know him."

"You can see how the earth is. They all left, one after the other, because they said it didn't pay. And now, you see what happens."

"Agathange knows him."

"So do I; people call him Panturle. His real name is Bridaine. He's a distant cousin of mine, on my wife's side."

"Whatever people say, that foreign wheat can't be compared with wheat from these parts. You see . . . "

And Monsieur Astruc ran about like a rat in spite of his big paunch, and he kept his hand in his pocket the whole time.

Behind the merry-go-rounds, over there under the lime trees, Panturle still remained. He was heavy and quite dizzy with that organ grunting like a dozen pigs. He was heavy, too, with all that money he had in his hand. Arsule stood against him, leaning against him, flushed with joy like the flame of a candle.

That was Panturle's wine: to feel her against him and happy. When there was nobody around, he put his arm round her waist, squeezed her a little to feel her supple and bending like a sheaf – and, in his other hand, he held the cash.

"Are you glad?" he said to her.

"I'd be hard to please if . . . "

"It makes a lot of money, doesn't it? How much would you say it makes?"

"Seven hundred and eighty."

"I've never had so much."

Then, they stood up and went into the fair. They had settled it like that. And until they mixed with the crowd, Panturle kept Arsule pressed against him with his arm around her, but as soon as they came to the booths, he pressed her to him one last time and then released her. Then they went on like two sedate people.

They stopped in front of Lubin's stalls.

"That man sells good stuff. You ought to buy yourself a pair of trousers and a coat."

"What about you?"

"Oh, me . . . "

"If you don't buy anything, I won't, either!"

"I'll see."

"I'll see too."

And they went by.

It nearly made them quarrel, because this happened in front of the shoes and all the other things. At last, Panturle took out the banknotes which he had placed against his breast, between his shirt and his skin, and handed them to Arsule. All of them.

"Here you are! Now do what you like with them."

All went well again like that. They bought the coat, the trousers, the shoes, two best-quality blankets of pure wool, a large basket closing with an iron rod, six handkerchiefs (three large and three small ones), a long rope, a whet-stone, three table knives, a saucepan, and a steam-cooker.

Then Arsule burst out laughing. She took out a ten-franc note and said:

"Will you give me this one?"

"You know I would give them all to you."

"No, but this one, I want it for myself."

"You've only to take it."

She laughed as she took it, then said:

"Wait for me, I'm going to buy myself something."

He stood and waited there, near the post-office. She left the fair and went down into the street leading to the main square.

After a while, she came back with a little parcel folded in tissue paper.

"Here you are," she said.

It was a beautiful, bright new pipe – the best of wood – and a pack of tobacco.

Tears rose to his eyes. He did not know what to say.

"You . . . you . . . " he said, as if to threaten her, as if to say: If ever

I catch you!

She was all puffed out with joy, like a pigeon.

"I knew you felt like one. And you see, I've got sixteen sous left."

It was true: there were sixteen sous left.

They might have waited for L'Amoureux. It was he who had carried the sacks for them in his cart and who had told them:

"At six o'clock be at the cartwright's and wait for me. We'll go back together."

But they had had enough of all the din, the music, the cries, the firecrackers, of all those people drinking, of all those tradesmen singing, and of the organ grinding away at full speed.

"It's all buzzing in my head," said Panturle; "if I had to bear it any longer, I'd go mad."

"So would I," said Arsule.

The truth was that they were longing to be alone in their own silence. They were used to big, open fields, slowly living their own life beside them. There, they were cemented, flesh to flesh, knowing in advance what the other was thinking about, knowing the word before it had left the mouth, knowing it even when it was still being formed with difficulty deep down in the breast. Here, the noise had cut them apart like a knife, and they had needed to touch each other by the arm or hand all day long to satisfy their hearts a little.

"D'you know what we ought to do if we were sensible? We'd start off at once on foot."

They set off by the Saint-Martin road. It was a short cut.

There was first a poplar, which started talking to them. Then there was the Saunerie rill, which politely accompanied them, rubbing itself against their road, hissing gently like a tame snake. Then there was the evening breeze, which caught up and went a little way with them, leaving them for the lavender, coming back, and then going off again with three large bees. Just like that. And it amused them.

Panturle carried the bag with all their purchases. Arsule, by his side, walked with a man's stride to keep in step. And she laughed.

Then night fell just as they came out of the wood and were about to slip down Aubignane vale. It was their old friend the night, whom they knew well and loved, night with her arms all wet, like a washerwoman, night bespattered with sparkling dust, carrying the moon.

They could hear the grasses breathe for miles around. They were at home.

Silence kneaded them into a single ball of flesh.

Just after the fair came three days of the kind that often come at the beginning of autumn. A plague, indeed! The weather played one dirty trick after another: first wind, then rain, then storms. The sky was like a cauldron. Besides, it was icy cold. After that, all that remained was a thick fog, white as milk. It was too wet to go out; one would carry the whole field under one's soles. Panturle stayed in the kitchen, making a handle for the screwdriver. Arsule had emptied the wardrobe. In the attic she had found a trunk full of newspapers dating from the turn of the century. With a pair of scissors, she cut paper festoons to put on the shelves.

"It keeps things clean, and it looks nice."

She was upstairs, in the bedroom. She could be heard coming and going. The fog was up against the pane. One could not even see the village. A crow could be heard through the fog, cawing. From time to time it could be seen flying in front of the window, like a shadow in the air. Apart from that, no noise, except the cracking of silence.

Panturle placed himself in the narrow ring of grey daylight flowing from the window. He had whittled down a piece of an oak branch, and was forcing it into the collar of the screwdriver.

But suddenly he lifted his nose and remained for a while listening with his hands disengaged. Then he turned slowly towards the door. As he turned, he was careful to set his feet noiselessly on the flagstones, and there he was now facing the door. His hand went for the big hunter's knife on the table. He caught the thick handle firmly in his fist, and the blade remained underneath, like a wet iris leaf. Without moving his head, he looked at the blade. All in order. It was there.

After that he silently took deep breaths.

Right. Something brushed against the door. Then somebody pushed the door slightly to look in.

Panturle understood all that because, since he had taken up the knife, his eyes had not left the big lever of the bolt, held in position by an iron catch. As the lever was a little loose, it moved without going up and clicked against the catch. Panturle glanced again at his knife. Then he looked at the ceiling. Upstairs, Arsule's steps could no longer be heard, but he caught the sound of a slight humming and it was a song he knew well. Good. She was in the bedroom, cutting her paper. All right. To get up, there were only the stairs. And he stood in front of the stairs, he, Panturle and his knife.

That seemed all right.

Now the lever of the lock started moving up slowly. Without noise, cautiously. The door was being pushed open. The fog from outside was already steaming in through the slit.

The door opened. A man stood on the threshold. When he saw Panturle, he stopped, with his hand on the door-knob. He was old.

"Isn't this Bridaine's house, here?"

"Yes," Panturle said.

"Good day," the man said.

"Good day," Panturle said.

"I've come, just to see if . . . Wait a minute, do you mind if I come in? It's rather cold outside."

"Come in, and shut the door."

Panturle did not let go of his knife, and watched the man. With a shiver the man pretended to tremble and tightened up his jacket.

"It's better in here."

"Yes. It's not bad. Are you alone?"

At that moment the man saw the knife.

"Oh!" he said. Then: "Yes, I'm alone, and you don't need that, Bridaine, I've not come as you imagine, and I'm not the sort of man you imagine. And that's a good knife. I know all about knives. I'm a knife-grinder."

"Oh! So that's what it is," said Panturle. A smile came under his moustache, and he put down his knife.

"Yes, that's it," answered the man.

Panturle made him sit down near the hearth, where the soup was simmering over quiet embers. He listened to him. The humming from upstairs could scarcely be heard. One had to know about it to hear it. Just as well.

The man looked slowly at the four walls, examining them one after another.

There, on the right one, there was a woman's fichu, hanging from a nail. He saw it. On the mantelpiece, there stood a row of canisters, well in order, the biggest in front, the smallest behind. On one side of the window there was a chair, with a pair of women's stockings hanging from its back; on the straw of the chair, there was a ball of darning-cotton, a wooden darning-ball, and a card of needles. He was not mistaken. On the other side of the window . . . but it was clear enough like that.

"Well, then," the man said, "I'd been asking for you, and was told: 'He's at Aubignane.' It was almost on my way. So I went out of it a little, and here I am. It doesn't make my way much longer; just a bit, but there's not much in it. Besides, I've something to tell you."

"Say it."

"You've never left this place, have you?"

"No."

"And you often go about the country, around here?"

"Yes."

The man stopped. What he wanted to say was not yet ripe.

He said:

"I've been through these parts once before, and came to this house, but there was nobody in.

"Anyhow, on that occasion, I was bothered all the time. It so happened, too, that I pulled a man onto the bank who was drowning in Chaussières hole."

"I know."

"You know?"

"Yes – it was me."

"It was you?"

His satisfaction was painted all over his face.

"Ah, good!"

He turned round, just to efface his joy, which was too conspicuous.

"Then it was you. That's good, because in that case you'll be able to tell me and explain something and I won't have come to Aubignane for nothing. It's like this, in a nutshell: since it was you, you'll know that at the time I was with a woman."

For a moment all that could be heard was two or three big rain drops pattering against the pane, because finally it had started raining again.

Panturle did not answer.

"As I was saying, I was with a woman. I am going to explain everything to you, so that you understand the situation. She was a girl I had picked up somewhere. We got on quite well together. But since that very night she's vanished like smoke. She melted away in the daylight. As for you, I can understand. You recovered when the night started to get cold, and you found yourself alone there, because you couldn't see us. We were sleeping under the willows. So you went away. That's quite natural. But what of her? I haven't been able to figure it out yet.

"Well, then, I wanted to ask you, just as I asked the others on the farms over there, if when strolling around or hunting, or somehow, you didn't happen to come across the woman, alive or dead or, at any rate, as you might say, it doesn't matter in what manner, but, just to know, because I naturally want to get to know somehow."

One could hear the rain against the panes.

He went on almost immediately.

"Because, I'll explain the situation and tell you the real truth about it. That woman, as I said, I picked her up just like that. I was at Sault, one day. She's not precisely the pick of the basket, not by any means. In fact, she's a trollop who could be picked up anywhere. I wasn't choosy – there was no reason why I should be, in my trade and at my age, and for the use I meant to make of her. Well, at any rate, that's how it was. She was a slugabed.

"Besides, as far as housekeeping goes, those women are always like that – not worth a fig. For instance, I'm fond of kidney-bean soup with a few potatoes and tomatoes, a small sprig of basil, and a dash of oil. It's not difficult, but she never brought it off once. That's how it is. She's a bit like a cat, you know, nestles snugly by anybody's fireside and sleeps there comfortably, but when it comes to working, she's never in a hurry!

"Then again, one naturally likes a bit of feeling. It doesn't cost much to say 'Thank you,' and it shows good breeding and one expects it. Well, as far as feeling goes, she might be dead wood or stone. You can give her all that she wants, be gentle with her, bring her this or that, and smooth out the day's work for her. Makes no difference. She's just like wood. She's got no more gratitude than a milestone. I had a dog once; well, I assure you I got more satisfaction out of him."

In the meantime Panturle got up, went to the table, took up his pipe and tobacco, then came back and sat down. He filled his pipe and packed it down with his thumb, then lighted it with an ember. He took the ember straight out of the fire with his fingers, held it to the tobacco, and drew with his cheeks. At last the smoke came, and after a while it became thick. The ember had grown black between his fingers.

After that the man stopped and waited. Panturle was looking at the bowl of his pipe.

"I'm telling you all this," the man resumed, "because it's the honest truth. If there is a word too much, let me be struck dead on the spot. But it sometimes happens in life that a thing you hear tell prevents you from being tricked. Because with creatures of that sort, the kinder you are, the sooner you are plucked. Then, as you'll agree, it's better to know a thing or two. Like that, when one's been warned, one's got to be a damned fool to be taken in. That's so, isn't it?"

Panturle was smoking. The rain stuck her slug-like belly against the panes. A gutter was spitting water near the stables. The man put his hand on Panturle's knees.

"There, mate, I've told you everything. It's for your good. I believe I saw you at the fair. And they told me you knew where the woman was."

Panturle drew back his knee. He took his pipe out of his mouth.

"Yes, I do know," he said. "She's here with me."

"Well, then?"

"Then nothing."

"After all I told you?"

"Yes."

They remained thus for a while looking at each other. Then the man's lips took on something like a smile, a little snake of a smile, which was cut into two by Panturle's voice.

"Yes, even after all you've told me, because it doesn't count, and" – he cleared his throat, for he also had a lot to say and some honest truths too, but once his throat was cleared, it was no longer worth speaking – "and there you are."

But all the same, he wanted to crush the smile for good and all.

"What does it matter to me? I've got two eyes and two ears, and two arms with two good hands, and I can use them alone, and I can look around me without anybody's help, and I know what I know.

"First of all, if she's as bad as all that, you must be quite glad to be rid of her."

"Yes, but she was my woman, and I fed her for two years."

Panturle laid his pipe on the hearthstone. He turned his chair, sat down with his big body right in front of the man, and began to look him straight in his eyes, without wincing. He remained thus for a moment, while the embers hissed and spat because of the rain falling down the chimney.

"So you fed her? For two years? That may be. But you, mate, have you considered a bit that she's given you two years of her life? Two years – and during those two years, did you think that she believed her life was over and the rest of her days would be the same as those she was living with you? Listen, don't get angry, we are here to talk it out, face to face. Because when I happen to hold something, usually I don't let it go unless somebody makes me do so, and to make me do so, one needs to be strong. Let's leave it at that. So you've thought a bit of what I've just said to you? It couldn't have been much fun to be with you. How old are you? You needn't reply. It's obvious.

"You understand me? In my opinion, it's paid."

The man was sitting there, wondering. He turned the words over in his mind. They were sound.

"It's all right," he said, "it's all right. I'm paid, as you say. You also say I'm old. Well, that's just what I wanted to talk to you about. I'm old. Well, that was mainly what I thought of when I took her with me. You don't know yet what it means to be old; I hope you'll know some day. Well, then, for me, she was a bit of a companion and, besides, I'd better tell you, she drew my cart."

He said no more. He lowered his head. He put his right hand on his left shoulder to feel the hard sore which the straps had planted there, and which sent its aching roots down his whole back.

"Buy yourself a donkey."

"It's a lot of money."

"All right," said Panturle slowly. "I'm not one of those men who steal other people's goods, and I like frank speaking. Listen. To tell you the truth, I was expecting you some day or other. You've come today; we'll settle today, and that'll be an end to it. You'll see."

He got up. When standing, he was as tall as the mantelpiece. He had only to stretch out his hand to take the little canister on which was written: "Pepper." He sat down again.

"Right. I'll pay for the donkey. But you must understand this: I'm replacing the woman with a donkey. Do you understand? I'm giving you enough to buy a donkey, there's an end to it."

He took a fifty-franc note out of the canister.

"Yes, but what about the harness," said the other, "and the tether, and all that? . . . Because I'll have to fit my hand-cart with shafts now . . . ."

"Right," said Panturle; "that'll be sixty, and that's that. You'll find as many donkeys as you like for thirty."

He held the notes at his fingers' end. Then he said: "Here you are," because the man was hesitating and still mumbling something under his moustache.

"Here you are."

The man took the two banknotes, he counted them: one, two. All right. He kept them in his hands a moment. Was it any good bringing the matter up again? . . .

No. He put them into his pocket. That was that.

"But you're going to sign me a paper," Panturle said.

"A paper? What for? It's not done for a thing like that."

"It can be done for anything. You'll write: 'Received sixty francs,' and you'll sign. Nothing more. That'll do. We'll both know what it means. Go ahead."

They made out the receipt. Gédémus had a pencil and he tore off a leaf from the notebook in which he wrote down his customers' accounts.

"Draw a line under 'sixty,'" Panturle said to him; "it must be seen clearly. There. What's written underneath?"

"Gédémus. That's my name."

"All right. Wait a minute, we'll have a drink on it."

And they drank each other's health with wine.

"Now I'm off," said Gédémus.

"Yes," said Panturle.

He accompanied him to the door. It had stopped raining. It had not been heavy rain. It was even sunny above the mist, and the grass glistened. Gédémus stopped on the threshold.

"All I've just told about the woman, you know . . . well, there's not a word of truth in it."

"I know," said Panturle.

He left the door open to make sure that he went. He was off. Silence returned. The branch of a lime tree was dripping into a bucket which had been left outside.

Panturle went back slowly to the table. He put the pepper can back on the mantelpiece.

A handle had to be put on the screwdriver.

Now that silence had returned, Arsule could be heard again upstairs humming to herself while tidying the wardrobe.

IV

AUTUMN PLOUGHING HAD BEGUN THAT MORNING. THE earth started to smoke with the first cut of the ploughshare. It was as if a fire had been discovered underneath. Now that six long furrows had been lined up side by side, the smoke over the field was as thick as from a bonfire of grass. It rose in the clear daylight and began to glisten in the sun like a column of snow. And it said to the crows slumbering on the wing in the wind from the plateau: "Ploughing's going on over there and you will find worms." Then they all came, one after another, sending full-throated calls to one another, and later in clusters like big leaves swept along by the wind. They hovered around Panturle, floating in the heavy air like flotsam around a ship.

It might have been about eleven o'clock in the morning when Panturle stopped to repair the tether which had just broken. And just as he raised his head on finishing the work, he noticed against the sun, which had now become warm, a man standing in Marius Aubergier's field. He was so surprised that he dropped the tether.

"Who can that fellow be?" he asked himself. Arsule was alone in the house. He had pressed heavily on the brake prop, driving the ploughshare deep into the earth. He had fixed the plough firmly at the end of the field so that the horse could prance around as it pleased without any risk. He was just going home when he saw the man coming down towards him. So he waited for him. But he left the horse and plough anchored, because he might need to have his hands free. One never knows.

The man came straight to him. He wore a small cap. The velvet of his corduroys was almost new. It could be heard rustling from a long way off.

On arriving at the first furrow, he bent down and took a little earth in his fingers. He looked at it, smelt it, played with it, and made it flow between his fingers, then looked at the earth rust that remained on his skin. After wiping his fingers on his corduroys he came forward.

"Well," he said, "is it going all right?"

"Not bad," Panturle replied.

Near at hand, one could see that he was slightly shorter than Panturle but strongly built, with good lines, shoulders well shaped, and firm hands.

"That's good earth, you know."

"Not bad," Panturle replied.

"I say that," the man continued, "because I'm going to be your neighbour. Yes. It's you, isn't it, who sold such fine wheat at the Banon fair? It is? Well, it's you who settled the matter. The wife had been saying to me for a long time: 'Let's settle on our own land, Désiré, and we'll be our own masters.' She'd been saying so for a long time, but we never managed to do it. The purse isn't fat and, as you know, those who've got land on the plain won't let it go. I've been farming a place near Mane. And I must say the wife's harping has been having its effect on me for a long time. So it all happened as if it were fixed up beforehand."

Panturle said to him: "You'll come and have a bite with us, but let me do three more furrows." And the man walked beside the plough while Panturle was finishing. He kept on bending down over the earth, taking handfuls and feeling the richness.

On entering the house, the man had an appreciative look for each object. The grey light was pleasant and soft as a cat's fur. It flowed through the window and through the doorway, bathing everything in its softness. The fire crackled in the hearth and used its red claws against the cauldron of soup, and the soup simmered and sizzled, producing a thick smell of leeks, carrots, and potatoes, which filled the kitchen.

With that smell it was as if one were already eating the vegetables. On the kitchen table were three fine onions completely peeled, which showed up in violet and white tints against the plate. There was a jug of water, a jug of clear water, and the pale, light sun was playing in it. The tiles had been washed. Near the sink, in a big crack which had split the stones and through which the earth could be seen, a green shoot of grass had grown, holding up its head full of seeds. (Arsule left it there for fun. She called it "Catherine" and talked to it while washing the plates.)

The man looked at everything, taking his time and considering each object carefully. He formed an opinion. And, once it was fixed, he said: "You've a good home here."

And even if he had not quite finished forming an opinion, he did so afterwards with Arsule's good soup.

First a soup plate full and brimming over, then another with all the vegetables whole, with leeks as white as fish, soft potatoes, and carrots; and the fine taste it all left in the mouth! They had a good slice of lean ham with a border of fat that shone like a piece of ice from a spring. After that they had cheese which had grown yellow between walnut leaves and was seasoned with little herbs. Then the man ate more slowly, because he began to have a full stomach and then because it seemed to him that with his mouthful he was crunching a piece of the hill itself with all its flowers. That completed his conviction and he said again: "You've a good home here, a good home!"

Then: "That's life!"

Then: "What a good housewife!"

Then: "We'll be neighbours, good neighbours whose likes will be found only here . . . . I'll lend you my mule. I've an American sower.

And you'll see . . . you'll see . . . ."

Then it was time for them to say "Good-bye," because for a while the man had said nothing, filled as he was with good food inside and good things to see outside. Panturle had started to think about his work again. Then it was time to go. The man shook hands with Panturle. He shook Arsule's little finger, for she had already begun washing and had wet hands. As he went, he said to them: "I'll see you in three days' time. You'll see the whole family. The wife's a good woman too. And the kids. You'll see. I've a boy and two little girls."

So they had to put up the whole family. It was a great time.

It must have been about four o'clock in the morning, in fact in the middle of the night, when they arrived.

The house was asleep. The first sign of them was shouts of "Hey, there!" which lasted quite a long while because the house was dead-asleep. Then they knocked on the door and Panturle got up. He took them into the kitchen. He soon had the fire alight. Arsule came down with only a petticoat over her nightdress, and her full bosom uncovered. Then, seeing people in the house, she covered herself.

Désiré's wife was called Delphine. She was a small stout woman, plump both in front and behind. She had a thick neck which seemed to have been made of lard, two sharp little eyes, and a good fruity mouth.

"Yes, Madame," Arsule said to her.

Delphine went three times to the trap and each time came back with a sleeping child in her arms. First she came with the youngest child, Madeleine, with her face puffed with good sleep just like an open rose.

Then came her sister Pascaline, with her head swinging behind like a marrow at the end of its stalk.

Then came little Joseph, who almost awakened. He opened his mouth and said: "Ho, there, cattle, get along!"

But it was in his sleep.

They laid them down on sacks. They prepared hot wine. Dawn came, then the day. By that time Désiré had unharnessed the mule and had sheltered it next to Caroline in the stables.

"The best thing," said Panturle, "would be to leave the women-folk here and for us two to go out. Then we'll come back and fetch them."

That is what they did, and Arsule and Delphine got to know each other fully in their own way, as women do. They talked first of one thing, then of another: of skirts, of preserved olives, of the price of shoes, of life's difficulties, and of how one mustn't complain too much. And they got on together.

The children awakened all amazed. There were bowls of goat's milk for all three, and Arsule brought these to them in a flutter.

Then the men came back: they were brothers. They had walked in the beautiful countryside and the morning flowed like a spring of gold.

The man said: "What we ought to do, Delphine, is to put up the children's beds and ours, and get the table in. The fireplace is good. As for cooking, he says we'll eat here at midday."

"Of course," Panturle interposed.

"Oh, no," said Delphine, "it'll disturb you."

But Arsule said: "Of course you'll eat here; I'll be overjoyed to have the children a little."

She did not leave the girls all day. The mother had work to do moving in, so Arsule took them for a walk in the fields. The little boy remained with his father and Panturle, who measured out the fields with big strides.

Arsule walked hand in hand with the two little girls all round the place. It was the finest day of that late autumn season. The air was sharp and clear, but the sun was still warm and there were no clouds. The flight of the thrushes could be heard among the juniper bushes. A russet hare stopped in astonishment in the middle of the moor, then with a big, low bound darted off along the ground. Crows called one another. The children looked for them, but could not see them distinctly. It looked just as if the big blue porcelain bowl of the sky were cracking. In the leafless hedges there were eglantine berries which had been nipped by the night frosts and were shrivelled and soft. Little Madeleine told Arsule that at

Mane they called them "bum-scratchers". All three laughed and Arsule said: "Wait till I scratch you, just you wait!"

They went down to the stream. It was all bearded with dirty grasses and was grumbling, for the rains had filled it with water. So it complained. It complained of being too fat. It was never satisfied. In summer it spent its time moaning that it was going to die, and then . . . Streams were always like that.

The little girls thus began their friendship with this new countryside.

There was a curlew calling in the bushes. They learned that when going down to Basse-Lande they had to wrap themselves up well in their shawls so as to protect themselves against the dampness. They learned that when they went towards the plateau the noise they heard was the wind, so they need not be frightened.

And Arsule petted them a great deal.

Evening came and a voice could be heard calling: "Pascali . . . i . . . ine."

They came back to the village.

Delphine had already made her nest.

The house in which she had put up was just in front of the sloping fields. As they went up, they saw the flame of the lamp.

"Well, won't you eat with us this evening?"

"Ah," said Delphine, "we must really get used to the place. If we begin by spending this evening in company, there will be nothing left for the long winter evenings. No, the house is ready. We'll stay here."

There was a fire in the hearth with flames more than a metre high, and the sound filled you with pleasure. Everything was already well arranged, swept and in order. There was little, but it was well placed. The shadow on the wall made up part of the furniture.

"Good night," said the little girls, holding up their faces.

Arsule went down alone. Up there the little girls were chattering. It might have been a magpies' nest.

"It's me," said Arsule, on coming home.

Panturle had made the soup.

"Now where are you going?"

"To see the goat," said Arsule.

She searched under Caroline's belly and, feeling among the warm hair, she took hold of a little kid. She sat down in the straw near the mother goat. She put the little kid on her knees. She stroked it. That walk had made her hungry for a child's caresses.

V

SPRING IN ITS FULLNESS HAD RETURNED. THE south had opened like a mouth. Its deep breath was blowing damp and warm, and the flowers quivered within the seeds, and the round earth began to ripen like a fruit.

The squadron of the clouds cast off their lashings, and one after another, in a long line, sailed up towards the north. The procession lasted a long while, and the earth could be felt swelling up with all those rains and with the reawakened life of the grass. Then at last, for good and all, the clear sky could be seen bubbling under the poop of the last cloud.

Yet a few sweepings of clouds were still left floating in the sky, clinging to the Aubignane steeple, just like a sheet held down by a stone in a stream.

That was how things stood: one dared not yet begin the labours of spring, take up the spade or the sack of seeds. One dared not make a start. It might rain again from one moment to the next. The great panting cloud was still above, clear, youthful, and the day was still quivering with lightning.

"Well, as long as the wind doesn't blow up . . . !"

Panturle was sitting near the hives under the cypress. He had set his idle hands on his knees. He was smoking. He watched the smoke. It uncoiled out of his pipe like a living being; it seemed to have body. It was because the air was still calm. The wind had not yet come.

He listened.

No – the wind had not yet come. It could not yet be heard pacing across the sky, but the south was all clean and it would soon come – perhaps that night, perhaps the next day.

"It was like that, on the evening that Mamèche went. And since then . . . If only she could see that . . . She could see it, or else there was no justice."

Désiré had repainted his shutters, and put a new door on his barn . . . . Delphine could be heard calling her little girls, then children's voices answered from the hedges. The two houses had velvety ploughed fields before their doors, spreading out like carpets.

Panturle was meditating. It was a clear day. Things could be seen easily. They appeared boldly and distinctly before the eye, and one could see the why and the wherefore. He saw order. It was obvious to him that the rubbish had to be emptied out on the other side of the lilac bush, and it was equally obvious that if the rubbish were not emptied out on the other side of the lilac, but there, for instance, or over there close by the little cherry tree, it would attract flies, and would smell unpleasant, and, besides, it would no longer be in order. He understood. It was good to have flattened out a threshing-ground and to have fitted the old stone-roller with an axle. It was good to have a small canister on the mantelpiece, even if the canister was marked "Pepper." It was good to have that canister ready in case there were an opportunity of buying a good mule. It might happen. He would wait and see. One could not always live by borrowing.

On the sloping path was Arsule with her pattens. They could be heard. Arsule was singing. Now she appeared from round the hedge.

She approached. She was dragging her feet slightly. As she walked she moved her shoulders a little as if to help her legs with all the strength of her body. She had become somewhat heavier, and somewhat slower. She was playing with a hawthorn twig.

He continued to watch her approaching. She was walking along the new grass, carefully choosing the places where daisies had not yet appeared.

Here she was.

"So you are here, at sundown?"

"Yes," he said, "I was thinking . . . ."

He looked at her with a new expression in his eyes. He noticed her ample body and her poise.

He stretched out his arm.

"Just stop a moment, girl."

Then:

"Come along, let me look at you."

She came up to him. He seized her by her curved haunches. She was like a jar in his hands.

"It seems as if . . . you were not so fat . . . ."

He held in his hands the bulging part of that jar which was of flesh. He looked at her searchingly from head to foot. She lowered her face, now full of a contentment as vast as the sky.

"Yes," she said, "now you know."

"Is it sure?"

"Without a shadow of doubt, it's already living; so much so, that the other night I felt it give me a kick, there . . . ."

She felt her side.

"You said to me: 'What's the matter?' I answered: 'Nothing.'"

He got up and put his arm on the woman's shoulder. There. She again felt on her shoulder that naked arm which weighed down like water.

"Girl . . . ."

There were so many things to say, that the best was just to say "Girl" and nothing more. And all that remained to be said could stay in the warmth of the heart, which was its place.

She added almost in a whisper:

"I keep on thinking of it, and it tickles me all over my hands, and on my lips, and I'm longing to have it in my fingers and to kiss it all over; wherever I can, everywhere."

After a moment, she continued:

"I'll have plenty of milk . . . . I feel my breasts sprouting."

Then again:

"At times I feel all dried up, like bark."

They stood silent for a long while, just breathing, against each other. And it was she who spoke again, as if after a dream:

"We'll both be in the grass . . . and I'll spurt my milk out to make it laugh."

A call reached them from the village:

"Pascali-i-ne!"

Delphine was looking for her little daughters.

"So will I," was all Arsule said.

Now Panturle was alone.

He had said:

"Girl, take care of yourself, go easy; I'll fetch water for you in the evening now; we're very happy together. Don't let's spoil things."

Then he set out with his big mountaineer's strides.

He walked briskly.

He was all wrapped up in his joy.

He was filled with songs, packed in his throat and pressing against his teeth. He puckered up his lips.

It was a joy of which he wanted to savour all the smell and taste the juice as long as possible, like a sheep eating grass in the evening among the hills. He went on like that, until the beautiful silence had settled within him and around him, like a meadow.

He came to his fields. He stopped in front of them. He bent down, picked up a handful of that rich earth full of air and seeds. It was an earth full of good will.

He felt all its good will with his fingers.

Then, all of a sudden, standing there, he became aware of the great victory.

Before his eyes passed the picture of the old earth, sullen and

121

shaggy with its sour broom and knife-like grasses. He suddenly realized what a terrible moor he had himself been, wide open to the great wild wind, to all those things that could not be fought without the help of life.

He was standing in front of his fields. He was in his big brown corduroy trousers, and it seemed as if he were wearing a piece of his ploughed fields. With his arms stretched down along his body, he stood motionless. He had won. It was over.

He stood firmly planted in the earth like a pillar.